"This was a mistake, Mr. Mantheakis."

"I think we're past formalities now, Princess."

"Why do you call me that?" Just the way he said "Princess" put her teeth on edge. He never used "Your Highness" or "Your Royal Highness," the proper title of respect.

"What would you prefer? Your first name?"

"'Your Highness' will do. And could you please put some clothes on?"

He smiled. Grimly. "Of course, Princess."

THE PRINCESS BRIDES

For duty, for money...for passion!

Discover three linked stories from rising star
author Jane Porter!

Meet the Royals—the Ducasse family:
Chantal, Niccolette and Joelle. Step inside their
world and watch as three beautiful, independent
and very different princesses find their
own way to love and happiness with
exciting, arrogant and *very* strong men!

The Princess Brides trilogy:

The Sultan's Bought Bride (#2418)

The Greek's Royal Mistress (#2424)

The Italian's Virgin Princess (#2430)

Available only from Harlequin Presents®

Jane Porter

THE GREEK'S ROYAL MISTRESS

THEPRINCESSBRIDES

HARLEQUIN®

TORONTO • NEW YORK • LONDON
AMSTERDAM • PARIS • SYDNEY • HAMBURG
STOCKHOLM • ATHENS • TOKYO • MILAN • MADRID
PRAGUE • WARSAW • BUDAPEST • AUCKLAND

ISBN 0-373-12424-4

THE GREEK'S ROYAL MISTRESS

First North American Publication 2004.

CHAPTER ONE

THE jet, part of La Croix's royal fleet, groaned and shuddered and Princess Chantal Thibaudet glanced up, her tea sloshing in her cup.

It'd been a relatively smooth flight until now. They'd been in the air for nearly three hours—almost halfway home to La Croix enroute from her week stay in New York—and although the princess's secretary and ladies-in-waiting were happily visiting in the back, Chantal was desperate to get home to her daughter again.

Yet she managed not to fidget, her expression remaining calmly neutral, too ingrained by years of public service to ever give away what she was truly feeling.

Chantal's lips curved slightly, fighting a self-deprecating smile. It still amused her—the vagaries of life. People didn't want to know the reality behind the palace doors. They wanted the beautiful hair and smile, the tiara, the stylish clothes. They wanted the fairy tale, not the truth.

The truth. Ah, the truth. Now that was something else altogether...

Chantal's smile faded and for a moment the bleakness of her future stunned her, the walls, the rules, the silence...it wasn't the life she thought she'd have. She'd always been so good, so earnest about everything, she'd been sure life would turn out differently.

Abruptly the plane dropped, a sharp somersaulting lurch that had Chantal's retinue giggling and glancing nervously around, checking other's reactions. Chantal herself skimmed the clusters of passengers. Her own skittish assistants, a couple members of the media, several men interspersed, executives, friends of the Thibaudets, airline personnel.

She hated rough flights. They were inherent in flying, and she'd grown up on airplanes, but now that she was a mother, Chantal dreaded takeoffs and landings and the rough patches of

5

air in between. Yet outwardly she feigned calm and took a sip from her cup.

No sooner had she lifted the cup to her lips than sound exploded from the back of the jet. The aircraft shook, a shiver like teeth chattering, metal scraping metal. The jet dropped yet again, a steeper descent, and suddenly the teacup saucer seemed miles away.

She didn't like this.

Uncrossing her legs, Chantal planted her feet firmly on the floor, doing her best to look relaxed. Unconcerned.

They weren't going to crash. It was just turbulence. Nothing serious. Planes hit pockets of turbulence all the time.

A flight attendant in the red and cream uniform of La Croix Royal airlines came hurrying toward her. "Let me take your cup," she said, swooping the cup and saucer from the princess. "We don't want to get you burned."

The plane was jolting now, great shudders like a silver belly dancer in the sky, and passengers were murmuring in the back even as Chantal's hairdresser began to cry.

Glancing up, Chantal's gaze met one of the male passengers. He was sitting not far, just across the narrow aisle in a matching leather chair, and his dark gaze continued to hold hers, his expression calm, compelling. He wasn't English, or French. He was too hard-looking, beautiful but hard, face all severe lines and planes—an uncompromising line of brow, nose, mouth, chin.

"It's bumpy," she said, raising her voice a little, compelled to make a connection. She didn't want to be afraid, hoped she didn't look afraid.

"Yes."

Chantal had the feeling that he resisted company—people. "Do you fly a lot?" she asked, trying to keep from thinking about the terrifying shimmying of the plane.

"Yes." His dark gaze was nearly as hard as the line of his cheekbone and jaw. "And you?"

"Quite a bit." She swallowed. But she'd never been afraid like this before. Her fear was intense. "I've never—" She broke off as the plane sank abruptly, and someone behind her screamed.

The hair rose on Chantal's nape and gripping the arms of her chair she concentrated on breathing. Be calm. Be calm. Be calm.

Heart racing, eyes burning, she turned and looked at the man across the aisle. She couldn't disintegrate. She had to remain focused.

Talk to him.

Make contact with him.

She drew a shallow breath, her head spinning. "You have an accent."

His black eyebrows dropped. "So do you."

Maybe he was Latin. Italian? Sicilian? The burning in her eyes turned to tears. She felt ashamed of her loss of control. "I'm from Melio," she said, naming her independent country off the coast of France and Spain.

"I'm from Greece," he said, suddenly rising. He crossed the narrow aisle, took the empty chair next to her.

Ah, Greek, she thought, even more unnerved by his close proximity. "I'm Princess Chantal Marie—"

"I know who you are."

Of course he did. How silly. She struggled to sound normal. Natural. "What's your name?"

"Demetrius Mantheakis."

Her lower lip quivered. Her throat felt swollen, a lump lodged right in the middle. "That's quite a mouthful."

His gaze held hers, eyes so intense they dazzled her. "Yes."

The jet groaned loudly and did a strange ripple as if it'd become serpentine. Flexible. Mobile.

Chantal's lips parted. She gasped in air. She turned to Mr. Mantheakis. "This isn't turbulence anymore, is it?"

"No."

She hadn't thought so, and she nodded, exhaling slowly, trying to ignore her fear, which had become a huge, tangible thing. The fear was cold and heavy, like that of breaking a sweat in the middle of a bad dream and wanting to wake, needing to wake, and yet being unable.

Demetrius leaned toward her, his broad shoulder bumping hers. "How's your seat belt?" he asked, but he didn't wait for her to answer. He reached over and checked the tension on her seat belt personally.

His actions said more than words ever could, and her fear grew, spreading within her. "You don't have to do this."

"Do what?" He stared at her, his dark gaze narrowed and focused on her face.

She thought his voice was like gravel, hard, sharp, and she found herself thinking his Greek accent wasn't like the Greeks she'd ever known. His tone was harder. His inflection harsher. "Entertain me. Distract me. Whatever it is you're doing."

"I call it company."

She tried to smile but couldn't. She felt wild on the inside, her heart pounding, her pulse racing. They were flying over the Atlantic Ocean, heading back to Europe. There was nothing below them but water. Even if they needed to land, they couldn't.

She turned to the window. The shuddering of the plane, the inky clouds, the sense that destruction was just a heartbeat away heightened her senses, time stretched endlessly so that the future was impossible—far, far out of reach.

Lilly.

She felt the acid at the back of her eyes. She pressed her knees tight to keep from letting tears form. Princesses don't cry. Princesses don't show emotion in public. Princesses must be above reproach.

But her daughter's face swam before her eyes, the sweet pale face, the fair hair, the little lips shaped like a Valentine.

She covered her face with her hands, rubbed her eyes, drying the tears before they could fall. She couldn't lose control. The captain hadn't made any announcement. The flight attendants were buckled into their jump seats but they looked quiet, focused, professional.

The jet shuddered and banked steeply left. Chantal sat forward as the plane continued to verve left. She glanced to her window again.

"I can't see anything," she said, the jet appearing to settle back into a more normal flight pattern. The world beyond her window was dark, thick with heavy cloud, and the plane sailed through the dense blackness shuddering every now and then as if to remind passengers that the danger wasn't over.

"It's dark out," he answered calmly, leaning back in his seat, his body relaxed, no tension anywhere in his big, powerful frame.

She wished she could take comfort in the fact that he was at ease, but his confidence shook her even more. "Can the pilots see?"

"They fly by equipment."

But what if their equipment was wrong, she wanted to ask? Instead she thought back on life, the choices made, the opportunities passed up. "Moments like these are great for self-analysis," she said with a brittle laugh. "Nothing like facing one's self."

"Regrets?" he asked.

Her eyes felt like they were on fire. "Dozens."

"Name one."

She shook her head, her hands gripping her armrests tightly. "There's too many. I can't think of just one, but all of them, all that life experience, all those hopes and dreams..."

"Life's never what you think it's going to be, is it?"

Her eyes sought his. He looked so big, so imposing and yet he projected strength. Calm. "No."

"What's turned out different for you?"

She gave her head a slight shake. She couldn't talk about this. She couldn't talk about anything.

Suddenly she flashed back to her weekend in New York.

She'd been the guest of honor of New York's annual Fashion Week, and the event chairs had booked her into the royal suite at the Le Meridien in New York, a sleek, glossy hotel with a strong French influence. She supposed they thought she'd be most comfortable with the French accent, but she hadn't come to New York to find France, or Melio, or even La Croix. She'd come to New York to find a bit of her past, at least her mother's past, but it hadn't worked out like that.

How could she ever find her mother, or even herself, in a posh hotel with sleek marble lobbies and even sleeker chrome and cherry wood restaurants and lounges?

But the hotel had been an interesting juxtaposition: all the white and black marble flanked by chrome and wood. The lounge was like that of a cruise ship with its enormous circles of light—portholes—and the small tables scattered tightly together reminded her of the tables on the deck, surrounding the pool. Life at the Le Meridien New York was crowded and upscale, chic and noisy, and maybe this was New York after all. Maybe the throb and hum of street noise mingled with clank of cutlery and surge of voices over the sweet bluesy voice of the singer—maybe this was exactly New York and maybe this was why Chantal knew she'd always be a stranger here.

This wasn't her island, her husband's kingdom, or her elegant and refined way of life.

But maybe that was New York's allure. She remembered her view from her royal suite, the view over the dark brooding cityscape with its Gothic-like points and steeples, soaring building, bright lights, water towers perched precariously on top of slim and squat towers alike. New York was about change, and choice, power and sacrifice, and as the city had pulsed around her and past her, she knew she didn't have that kind of strength. Or courage.

"Life's a puzzle," she said softly, still thinking of her week in the city, and all that she'd seen and heard. Places like New York and London reminded her that there were so many different people in the world, and so many ways of doing things.

"It can be. Or it can be quite straight forward."

It'd once been quite straightforward for Chantal, too. But not anymore. Not since her marriage, Lilly's birth, Armand's death. Nothing was clear. Or simple. And thinking of the lack of simplicity reminded her of her waiter just that morning in the hotel's restaurant. She'd had her own table—her personal secretaries and valets seated at one nearby—and her waiter defied description. Literally.

"There was a waiter at the hotel's restaurant," she said slowly, picturing the tall waiter, who had to be at least six-foot-one or -two, and had long hair, a soft voice, sloping shoulders, soft waist, full hips, and yet, he was a man. At least he'd been born a man. "The waiter didn't fit his body. I don't know if he'd been taking something to become more feminine, or maybe he was simply willing it, but..."

"But what?"

"I admired him." Chantal looked up, into Mr. Mantheakis's eyes, and she felt her insides wrench. "I admired him for refusing to spend his life as someone, or something, he didn't want to be...for being unable or unwilling to spend the rest of his life in a body that didn't fit, or playing a role that didn't suit."

"Seems the waiter took drastic measures."

"I think he was brave," she whispered, breaking the gaze, turning to glance out her window at the darkness surrounding the plane.

In the restaurant this morning she'd been first puzzled, then confused, and finally sympathetic. And her deep sympathy made her feel an ounce of the pain he must have felt to have changed his world so.

She knew what it was like to start out as one thing and to battle it constantly. To struggle through the days, to deny the natural impulses again and again, to order oneself to do it because...because.

"Coffee?" the waiter had asked her this morning, with a voice that was pitched soft like a woman's and yet still distinctly male.

The waiter's voice had buried deep in her heart where she tried not to let emotion go. She'd felt such empathy for him that she tried to smile, and yet her eyes filled with tears. This poor man must have endured years of pain. "Please," she'd said, forcing herself to speak, and looking up, she'd met the waiter's eyes, and smiled, really smiled, even as she thought that no one got through life without tremendous pain.

"But you're brave." Demetrius Mantheakis's voice brought her attention back to him. "You've done incredible things in your life."

She shook her head, the memories of the morning still burning inside her heart. "No. Not like that. I've never really fought for anything." And suddenly her voice broke and Chantal closed her eyes, wishing she could disappear. She didn't want to feel this much. Didn't want to think this much.

"If you could do it over, what would you fight for?" he persisted.

Chantal stirred uncomfortably in her seat. She wanted off the plane. She wanted away from this man who asked hard questions and wanted real answers. It'd been a long day, but she didn't know how not to answer him. There was something forced in him, something about him that compelled her to speak. "Happiness," she said at last.

"Happiness?"

Her shoulders lifted, fell. She couldn't believe she was telling him this...sharing this. "I never thought it'd be so elusive. I always thought we'd all have an equal shot at it."

"And you didn't?"

She never talked to people like this, and yet now that she'd started opening up, she couldn't seem to stop. It was as if he'd unleashed a storm inside of her. "I don't know what went wrong. I tried so hard to do the right thing, and I always thought, if you just try hard enough, just be good enough, honest enough, kind enough, compassionate enough...if you work hard enough and give enough you'll discover that elusive happiness that others seem to have. You'll find happiness and—" She broke off took a breath, the aching emptiness inside her like a live thing, humming.

Deep grooves formed at his mouth. "And what?"

"Peace." *Peace.* She didn't close her eyes but on the inside she felt so weary and empty that she would have if he hadn't been watching her so closely. But he doesn't know you, she reminded herself, he knows your name, but that's it. He'll never really know you. And even if you survive this crazy flight— something that looked decidedly remote at the moment—they'd never see each other again. Was there really that much harm in opening up? Being honest? Speaking from the heart?

Her entire life had been dictated by duty, country, economy. As the oldest of King Remi Ducasse's three grandchildren, she was destined to be the future queen and monarch of Melio. She'd known since her teenage years that it was her duty to marry well, provide heirs, secure financial stability and guarantee independence from their powerful neighbors Spain, France and Italy.

To speak from the heart. To live according to the heart. These were not choices she'd been allowed to make. Her heart had long ago been overruled by her head and her innate loyalty and desire to do right had long ago eclipsed impulse and sentimentalism. There was that which was right, and there was that which needed to be done, and she knew when she married one day she'd marry a suitable match, a match arranged by her grandfather and his advisors. She'd bring prosperity back to their tiny kingdom, and stability.

That was her job. It was the job she'd do.

And it was the job she'd done. Tragically the moment she married Armand, Chantal knew she'd made the worst mistake of her life and having Lilly only made it worse.

But just thinking of her young daughter made her smile on the inside. Lilly was everything. Absolutely the greatest, purest joy life could bestow. A gift. A reward. A lifeline.

Suddenly the plane groaned again, metal scraping, the body of the jet rippling now as if in agony.

Chantal clenched her hands in her lap as the lurching plane shivered and shrugged as if struggling to molt its gleaming silver skin.

What was going to happen to Lilly?

She knew her brother-in-law, King Malik Nuri, the sultan of Baraka had been working on freeing Lilly, trying to find a way to escape the archaic La Croix laws, but so far nothing had worked, which meant, if the plane went down, or broke apart, or did whatever it was that planes do, then Lilly would be trapped forever with the Thibaudets in La Croix. Chantal couldn't bear the thought. The Thibaudets, Armand's parents, were cold and hard and they would control every choice, every thought, every breath Lilly took.

Her head spun. Her stomach heaved. She was going to be sick.

From nowhere a hand pressed to the back of her head, forcing her down, urging her face to her knees. "Breathe."

Demetrius Mantheakis's touch was firm and yet his voice was calm.

With his hand against the back of her head, and her nose bumping her knee, she felt utterly bewildered by the turn of events. Earlier today she'd been in New York, wrapping up her trip and missing Lilly dreadfully, and now she was getting ready to say goodbye...

Eyes squeezed closed she fought for control. You have to be okay, you have to be able to let go. No one lives forever...no one gets forever...

"Breathe," the voice above her commanded again.

"I can't." Her voice broke and the tears fell onto her knees. "I can't—"

"You can. You must. Come on, Chantal, be tough."

His hard voice was like a slap, right, left. After a moment she felt calmer. She was breathing again. More deeply. More regularly.

"I'm fine now," she said, and she pushed up, against the weight of his hand.

Little by little he let go of the back of her head.

Sitting upright, she tried to meet his gaze but couldn't. Demetrius Mantheakis scared her almost as much as the shuddering plane.

Demetrius watched the princess knowing that they were in trouble, knowing that he was calm because there wasn't a great deal either of them could do now. They were either going to make it, or they weren't going to make it. Either way he'd be with Princess Thibaudet. If they survived he'd be there. If they died, he'd be there. He could afford to be calm. Certain decisions were already made for them. It was a matter of waiting.

"I'm fine now," she said again, and this time her voice was deeper, calmer.

He studied the way she sat in her chair, her hands clenching the armrests. "There's nothing wrong with being afraid." He saw her head jerk up, her blue gaze meeting his. Emotion darkened her eyes, etched fine lines around her soft mouth.

"Are you afraid?" she whispered.

"To some degree, yes."

Chantal looked away, her fingers pressed to the cool metal armrests. She wasn't a little afraid. She was very afraid, and for the first time in years she only wanted the truth. Just the truth.

Save the promises and the pretense and all the flowery phrases people were always trying to give her. "Are we going to make it?"

"We're going to give it our best shot."

Demetrius's steady voice made her want to scream. He was so fixed, so contained while she felt absolutely sick with fear. If it weren't for Lilly then she could go, she could say goodbye, she could accept that she'd had her turn, lived her life, but there was Lilly and Lilly needed her.

God, give me sixteen years, Chantal prayed, *I want sixteen years. Sixteen more years for birthdays and hugs and conversations late into the night about anything and everything Lilly could possibly want to discuss.*

I won't ask her to live for me. I won't ask her to be anything for me. I won't ask her to become anyone but Lilly. I just want to be there for her. I want to open doors for her, and then tuck her in late at night, knowing she is home, knowing she is safe.

Chantal flexed her fingers, dug her nails into her palms. "If I don't make it home—"

"You'll make it home."

She wanted to believe him, she really did. "But if I don't, promise me you'll tell my daughter—"

"*Chantal.*"

His hard voice, fixed, like a slab of rough hewn marble, dragged her gaze up, all the way up from his chest to his open collar to his chin and jaw and mouth. Once her eyes met his, she felt cold and hot, a tangle of live nerves. "You don't call me, Your Highness."

"But you're not my highness. You're Chantal Thibaudet—"

"I hate that name." She grew even colder, ice crystals all over her heart. "I am not Thibaudet. That was my husband's name."

"And he died."

She swallowed convulsively. "And he died."

"And you're not going to die."

"No."

His lips curved into the faintest glimmer of a smile. It was like a black wolf. Teeth bared. "That's the first positive answer I've heard from you."

"And that's the first smile I've seen from you."

"I don't like smiling."

She laughed. For a moment, as incredible as it was, she forgot the shuddering plane, the dips and lunges in space, the wretched nausea pervading every limb. "You don't like smiling?"

"Fools smile."

Chantal choked on her muffled laugh. "You must be joking."

His head cocked, his dark eyes met hers and the feral intensity in his eyes made her shiver inwardly, a shiver that had nothing to do with the plane and fear, and everything to do with awareness.

Like Armand, he possessed tremendous confidence. But she knew what happened with men like Armand. They decimated those around them, tearing into them, bite by bite until nothing remained. No spirit. No self-esteem. No sense of self.

Her laughter died in her mouth, strangled in her throat. Hard men, strong men weren't the kind of men she wanted to know.

The jet suddenly plunged down, a steep free for all, and somewhere behind Chantal a woman screamed, a long terrified cry that seemed to go on and on as the jet hurtled toward the ocean below.

Demetrius's hand reached out, covered hers, held her fists tightly in his. "I'm here."

She gripped his hand with all her might. "We're going down."

"We're going somewhere fast."

There was an edge to his voice now, a hardness that spoke volumes. He felt the urgency, and the peril. He was meeting her where she was. Two human beings...mortals...no distinction between anyone now.

"Thank you," she choked, her mouth all sand, her heart beating so hard her eardrums sounded as if they'd explode. "Thank you for doing this. Being with me."

"My pleasure."

Yellow masks dropped.

Chantal stared at the bright yellow cup swinging in front of her, and then she remembered all those flight briefings, all those routine instructions. She reached for the mask, pulled it over her head, settling it on her nose. The mask fit.

She turned, looked at Demetrius. His mask was in place. His eyes creased.

Her mouth trembled. Tears filled her eyes. "I want to go home."

"To your daughter."

She nodded, hands gripping the arms of her chair so tightly she thought the bones would snap.

"Tell me about her," he said, his voice coming from very far away. "How old is she? What's her favorite color?"

Chantal blinked, dragged in air, felt tears well. The jet was in a downward spiral and he was trying to keep her from falling apart. Trying to keep her mind occupied. "Four." The pressure in her ears, the pressure in her head was intolerable. She blinked, head spinning, ears feeling as if they were going to burst. "Green." Blinking dizzily, Chantal dragged in another excruciating breath. "Her favorite color is green."

The plane was tumbling, spinning, and her seat belt strained, pulling tight across her lap, barely holding her into her seat. With a thud she felt Demetrius's arm strain against her chest, battling to pin her back into her seat. "What's she like?" he demanded.

Chantal couldn't focus. The pressure in her head made her want to scream like the others in the back who were crying out for God and help and deliverance. *Shy.* She closed her eyes. *Lilly's shy.*

Her blood was pooling in her head, in her ears and she knew she couldn't withstand much more pressure.

Lilly.

She pictured Lilly, kept her daughter's face before her, held love for Lilly in her heart. And as the world spun past, Chantal realized for the first time that love couldn't be contained. Love isn't trapped or shaped inside the body but is alive throughout the universe.

Love is inherent in every living organism, every cell, every creature and man.

Lilly would be fine.

Lilly would have Aunt Nic and Aunt Joelle, she'd have Grandfather and Grandmamma and there would always be the people in Melio who'd love her, embrace her, accept her.

She'd be fine.

A voice sounded on the jet's speaker. The captain announced that they were going to attempt to land. "Brace yourself."

Brace yourself. For the worst. For the best. For the rest of your life.

Demetrius's arm was now forcing her head down again, shaping her into a ball. "Hold on."

I love you, Lilly.

"Hold on," Demetrius ground out yet again, his hand in a death-grip against the back of her head.

I'm holding.

CHAPTER TWO

FOR a moment nothing happened. They were still flying-floating-hanging suspended and then in the next moment they bore straight down, down, down, gravity and turbulent air rushing at them in a frenzied battle that left her gasping for breath.

Then the ground came up at them, grabbing for them as if two giant arms were reaching up into the sky. The jet slammed against the earth. Bounced. Slammed down again. Bounced up higher, metal exploding, popping, screeching until Chantal was sure they'd be consumed by the heat and metallic noise, the smell of burning rubber and gas.

A plume of black smoke filled the cabin and as smoke poured into the cabin, the jet skidded sideways, a runaway plane sliding into the night.

The jet's momentum carried them along, and inside the battered plane they were being thrashed about, thrown to the right and left, narrow seat belts barely restraining.

Something bright flared, color, light, heat. Fire.

The plane was on fire.

But the jet was still moving, still sliding, still racing along like a giant's plaything, until the body snapped apart, nose gone, tail falling away, the belly sawing open.

Dazed, Chantal saw the night sky overhead. Blinking, she tried to focus on what must be stars even as something warm and wet dripped on her from above. She drew a shallow breath, finding it hard to breathe. Everything was so hot, the air so thick and steamy. Smoke and petrol burned her nose and she gagged a little. Had to get this mask off. Had to get out of here.

A hand groped at her waist, reaching for her seat belt. Stupidly she tried to rise but her legs wouldn't hold her. It was like coming off one of those carnival rides, the spinning teacup one that threw equilibrium to the wind.

Again Chantal tried to rise, but her chest hurt, her legs trembled. Her body refused to cooperate even as her mind screamed. Have to get off. Have to get out.

Her face was wet, sticky. Must be raining. Or was that acrid burning smell petrol?

"Take my hand," a voice commanded. Demetrius's voice, she dimly registered. But she couldn't seem to find him, or his hand, and she turned weakly in her seat, stared back behind her, realized that the others were gone, that the tail of the jet was somewhere behind.

"*Chantal.*"

He said her name so harshly that her head jerked back. He was standing and she stared at him in shock. His face looked blurry. Only his dark eyes made sense. They were fierce, black.

He pulled her to her feet and Chantal tried to move but her legs were soft, pillowy, the strangest weakest sensation. "I smell fire," she said, her voice eerily calm.

"The tail section is burning."

"Where is it?"

"Behind us."

She nodded, accepting this, and with her hand in his she tried to follow him across the pale taupe carpet with the bold gold and black border. Funny how the carpet looked the same.

But then the carpeted aisle ended abruptly, falling off away, and a huge scrap of silver sheet metal jutted up, twisting into the sky like a postmodernist garden sculpture. "Careful."

Again his voice was hard, ruthless and she nodded. There were no words left, no thought in her mind. She would have followed him anywhere at that moment.

He jumped down first, then lifted her from the carpet into his arms.

"I can walk," she protested as he carried her away from the tangled wreckage.

"You're bleeding."

Her head fell back, she stared into his face. His jaw was set, his expression ferocious. "I'm not bleeding."

He didn't answer. He just kept walking, carrying her as if she were nothing, moving swiftly to an unseen point in the distance.

From nowhere a siren sounded in the warm heavy darkness, the mournful siren piercing the humid night.

Thank God. Help's arrived. Gratefully Chantal closed her eyes.

With the princess slumped against his chest, Demetrius carried her from the burning plane to the clearing up ahead. He intentionally was taking her away from the other survivors who were gathering away from the wreckage. He was glad she'd passed out. He wasn't in the mood to talk, or try to explain what had happened.

He'd failed. Plain and simple.

He'd been hired to protect her. And he hadn't protected her. Regardless of the circumstances, he took full responsibility for the crash. The crash should have never happened.

He'd swapped flight crews, substituting the cockpit flight crew for his own. He'd changed flight attendants, too, unwilling to take the chance that the danger would come from one of those that were paid to serve the princess. He'd done his best to screen all those traveling with Chantal, and he'd felt reasonably confident that those flying with her were loyal.

In the end, the problem had been the jet itself. He'd had it inspected. Obviously the inspection hadn't been thorough enough.

You'd think after ten years he would have learned something. He got into this line of work by default. There'd been a breech in family security and he'd paid the ultimate price. The tragedy had turned him into a vigilante, and later a security expert. He was too ruthless, too cold to be a good bodyguard, which was only one of the reasons why he didn't take personal assignments, but after King Nuri of Baraka, Princess Chantal's new brother-in-law, had explained the situation to him, Demetrius couldn't say no. His company routinely provided high profile, celebrity security detail, but Princess Chantal Thibaudet's situation was different.

Widowed at twenty-seven, she was a stunning member of the royal family with a four-year-old daughter and someone wanted her gone. Dead.

The maliciousness of the intent, as well as the fact that a young child would be left orphaned, made his blood freeze. The widowed princess was far too visible, and far too vulnerable.

After studying the files, Demetrius knew he couldn't refuse the job. King Malik Nuri and the elder Ducasse royals didn't know how to handle this sort of threat. But Demetrius did. When it came to offering the dirtiest form of protection and intimidation, Demetrius was on a level of his own.

He didn't mess around.

He usually didn't make mistakes.

He'd made one today and he'd never forget it. The princess and her family could damn well believe he wasn't going to make another mistake, not when it came to her safety, nor her daughter's future.

The ground grew soft beneath his feet and the voices and cries of the passengers faded with the distance. They'd found land in the middle of the Atlantic—God only knew how the flight crew had managed to do that—he owed them hugely. They'd be compensated.

He heard a dull roar, the endless, monotonous sound of water against sand. Apparently the jet had landed within a couple hundred feet of the ocean. If they'd overshot the runway even a little bit, they would have broken apart in the water. Another miracle.

Demetrius crouched down, set Chantal in the still warm sand. He checked her vitals as best as he could and she seemed fine. It was the bump on her head that worried him. Part of the upholstered wall in front of them had come flying back at them.

He wished he had a flashlight. He wanted to check her eyes, see if they were as dilated as he feared.

She stirred, lunged forward. *"Lilly?"*

The terror in her voice cut him. "She's fine, Chantal." He wrapped an arm around her to keep her still. "Lie back, relax."

"Where is she?"

"Home."

Her expression cleared and she drew a slow breath. "She wasn't on the plane."

"No."

Her eyes closed. "Thank God." She drew another breath and

her eyes opened. She looked at him in the dark. He could see the whites of her eyes, the glimpse of white teeth as she bit her lip, organizing her thoughts, controlling her emotions. "We made it."

"We did."

She swallowed. "And the others?"

"I know there were survivors. I saw quite a few passengers gathering outside the wreckage."

She struggled to free herself. "We should go. We need to be there. I should be there." Her voice sounded hollow. Numb. She was in shock, probably had no idea what she was even saying. "I need to go help. People are hurt—"

"Can't."

"I must."

"It's not safe."

"Why?"

He stared at her for a long moment, before shaking his head, expression grim. "Too volatile."

She frowned, bemused. "The plane, you mean?"

"Among other things," he said, gently releasing her and watching her settle back on the soft sand.

The sand felt surprisingly warm beneath her and pressing her knuckles into the fine grains, Chantal's brow creased. Were they really still alive?

It seemed impossible. Improbable.

Eyes narrowing, heart pounding, she struggled to focus on Demetrius's face and process his words. It had sounded as if he were speaking in a megaphone—loud but not clear—and she struggled to understand why her hearing was off, why he sounded so far away when he was standing so close.

Gingerly she reached up to touch her forehead where it throbbed. It hurt to lift her arm, and her fingertips came away crusty when she touched her temple. She probed a little more and felt something gummy, still warm and sticky. Blood.

She must have hit something pretty hard then. Odd. She didn't remember hitting anything, but in the moments when the plane had been on a collision course with the earth, everything seemed to fly at her—a leather purse, a high heel, a paperback novel. It was as if they were in outer space: astronauts operating in zero gravity.

"Did you ever lose consciousness?" she asked tiredly, wiping her hand on her short suit skirt. Somewhere along the way she'd lost the matching woven pink and mossy-green jacket.

"No."

She nodded. She felt so strange. Almost otherworldly. How could they have survived what they did? "And you're not hurt?"

"No."

Again she nodded; thinking that time had changed, evolved, become almost 3-D. She could see them on the jet, could feel the terror still, could taste the smoke and blood and fear, and yet here they were, on some remote island off where? In the middle of the Atlantic? "Where are we?"

His thickly built shoulders shifted. "Off the coast of Africa, I believe."

"It's impossible. There was no land..."

"Our excellent flight crew found some."

Chantal gave her head another bemused shake. She felt as if she'd been through the spin cycle on a washing machine but they were *safe*. Alive. "Where's the plane?"

"Over there." He gestured inland, back to the thickly forested land behind them. "Everyone's just on the other side of the trees."

"We're that close to the water?"

"We very nearly parked offshore."

She didn't know why, but his expression, his dry tone, even the words he used, made her smile faintly. "We're lucky to be here."

"Very."

Nodding numbly, she stared off into the distance, seeing the endless line of dark water, feeling the heavy humidity in the air, the glance up into the sky, which revealed a half-hidden moon.

She couldn't absorb it all.

The danger was still so recent, so real, she couldn't quite believe they'd come through relatively unscathed. And then her heart tightened. What about the others? She had to know about her attendants, her staff. Most of the young women that worked for her weren't married yet, but they were still someone's daughter, sister, girlfriend. She had to check on them. Had to know the facts.

She struggled to rise, the effort making her body throb. She hurt. All over. "I need to get back to the plane."

"No."

Teetering to her feet, she ignored him, just as she ignored the pain pulsating hot and sharp around her lower ribs. "I'll never forgive myself if they're hurt and I sat here doing nothing."

He rose and settled his hands on her shoulders. Firmly. Heavily. He held her immobile. "I can't let you go back."

"You don't understand—"

"I do." And then suddenly he pressed a finger to her lips, silencing her. "Shh. Someone's coming."

His gaze was fixed on the grove of trees behind them and he touched his side, just beneath his arm. She knew the gesture. Her secret service detail had done the same thing numerous time before. He was checking for a weapon. A firearm.

He carried a firearm?

Demetrius was moving in front of her, shielding her. "Who's there?" he called.

A male voice replied in Greek.

Demetrius relaxed slightly, but not much. She felt the power in his body, his broad back tight, muscles hard, ready. He spoke to the other man rapidly, his voice deep, short, no-nonsense.

He was a man accustomed to being obeyed.

Chantal glanced up at him, took in the back of his head, the width of his shoulders and wondered who he really was and what exactly he was doing on her plane.

The man by the trees faded back into the darkness and Demetrius drew her down onto the sand. He sat close to her. "You can rest easy now," he said roughly. "That was the pilot. There are some injuries, no casualties."

She felt an almost dizzying wave of relief. "You're certain?"

"Everyone's been accounted for, and while some of the injuries aren't pretty, none appear life threatening."

"Thank God."

He nodded. "They've radioed for help. We're going to stay here until help arrives. It's safer."

She wanted to ask, how was it safer? But she didn't have the strength, or energy. She was tired. Sore. She thought she'd do just about anything for a couple of aspirin. Maybe it was better to sit, and rest. She felt as if she could sleep for months. Years. "Okay."

"Okay."

And some of the weight rolled off her shoulders. Her head felt a little lighter. The worries less agonizing. There was nothing she needed to do. Nowhere she needed to go. She could just sit here and be.

How strange. How wonderful.

Time passed. Slowly. Chantal felt drowsy and yet she struggled to keep her eyes open. As the hour passed, a warm wind picked up, banking heavy clouds overhead and sweeping the sand into whirling dervishes.

"Follow me," Demetrius said, taking her hand and pulling her to her feet.

She winced as he tugged on her arm. Her ribs were really sore.

He found a spot on the beach he liked. The position faced the water, was backed by a high hard dune, and provided an unobstructed view of the forest and the clearing. If anyone approached, he'd see.

Gathering some fallen branches from the forest, a few palm fronds, several fragrant eucalyptus branches, he built a miniature lean-to into the sand dune. It didn't take him long to put the shelter together, but by the time he was done, dark storm clouds had virtually obscured the white moon.

"It's going to rain," she said, frowning up at the now nearly black sky.

He nodded, and watched her gingerly creep backward into the lean-to, her lips pinched, her face a study in concentration. She was hurting.

He'd felt her tense as he drew her to her feet a few minutes ago, and he'd thought perhaps she was simply stiffening up. Maybe she was. But it could be more serious, too.

He didn't want to confront her, or risk offending her unless he absolutely had to, but he'd been hired for a job and he'd do his job. He took a seat next to her in the little shelter, the warm sand against his back. "Why don't you take your shoes off, Princess? You might as well get comfortable."

She glanced at her high heels. They were the palest pink suede banded by a darker pink leather trim. Biting her lip, she bent down to slip one shoe off and then the other. As she tugged each heel off, her lips pinched again, a needle of pain between her brows.

"Where does it hurt?" His deep voice sounded harsh even to his own ears.

"I'm fine."

"That's not what I asked."

Her fine dark eyebrows furrowed with displeasure. "Pardon me?"

She sounded positively imperial and frigid, shifting into the glamorous and untouchable Thibaudet Princess. "You're hurt," he said bluntly.

"No."

"You wince every time you move."

"A little bruising, Mr. Mantheakis."

She was trying hard to put him in his place, but she didn't know that he didn't believe in a caste system. He'd come too far to subscribe to class, status or social pecking order. In his world, people were people. Period. "It's worse than that."

"It's not." She averted her face, tilted her small straight nose higher, and yet he saw her hands burrow deep in the sand.

She might want to project cool indifference, but she was suddenly afraid. Afraid of him. She wanted to leave, to return to the others.

Terrifying her would solve nothing. He sought to gentle his voice. "I need to check for injuries."

"Absolutely not."

"It won't hurt."

She drew a deep breath, her nostrils flaring. The wind rustled through their small shelter, tugging at the princess's hair, catching one long tendril and blowing it across her cheek.

She caught the curl, and forced it back behind her ear. "I want to return to the plane."

"You know we're not going to do that."

Chantal attempted to rise but Demetrius's arm wrapped around her, pulling her back against him.

She inhaled sharply as she felt the heat of his body through his shirt, the hard planes of his chest against her back. "Let me go."

"I'm not going to hurt you."

His deep voice sent shivers through her and she felt a sob form inside her chest. He was so much stronger than she was. He was completely overwhelming her...dominating her. "You've no right to touch me."

"You're making this harder than it has to be."

She closed her eyes, turned her face away, her cheek grazing his chest. She felt the smooth thick muscle of his shoulder, felt the warmth of his skin and the even thud of his heart.

He was strong. Very strong. It crossed her mind that nothing invaded these walls of his arms. He was a power unto himself. Law.

Like the ancient Greek warriors and conquerors, the Greeks that founded civilization, changing the world forever.

"Please let me go," she whispered, a new fear welling.

"After I make sure there are no other injuries."

"There are none. Trust me."

"Can't take your word for it, Princess. Sorry."

Her breath was coming more rapidly, and opening her eyes she looked up at him, into the hard edges of his face. His cheekbone was high, almost too high, giving his face a harsh angle, and his chin, blunt cut, did nothing to ease the arrogant lines.

Pulse quickening, she knew he wasn't someone she wanted to negotiate with. "I haven't broken anything."

"I have to check you anyway—"

"*No.*" He was mad, out of his mind. "No, no, no, and no." There was no way she'd let his hands go anywhere on her body. "I'd know if I'd hurt something—"

"You didn't know you were bleeding."

"I thought it was rain."

"Exactly." He shifted, placed her on the ground and he crouched in front of her.

She avoided looking at his chest and her gaze settled on the taut muscles of his thighs, his trousers snug around his quadriceps.

"If you'd unbutton your blouse, Princess."

She nearly choked on her tongue. *"Mr. Mantheakis."*

He didn't reply. He was waiting. And he was patient. Very patient. Patience alone gave him tremendous strength.

Chantal felt a stirring of genuine panic, sensing she'd lost power, considerable power. "I'm not about to take my clothes off. I'm wearing very little as it is."

"I'm only asking you to unbutton your blouse. It's not as if you're naked under your blouse. You're wearing a bra."

Naked. Bra. Blouse. This was *her* body they were discussing, her clothes, her privacy. "Yes, but—"

"Do I need to unbutton your blouse for you?"

"Don't you dare. You've no right, no—" She broke off, startling when his hands reached for her, fingers brushing the full curve of her breast. *"Stop!"*

"I'm not in the mood to argue."

"Back off."

"Be quiet."

Chantal's jaw dropped. My God, another Armand. These insufferable arrogant boorish males were everywhere. She slapped at his hand. "I might be a silly thirty-year-old princess, but I'm not a complete fool. You don't have to take my blouse off to check for broken bones. You can inspect for damage through my blouse just as well."

"I'm looking for deep contusions."

"Thank you very much, but I have my own doctor in La Croix."

"We're going to be here all night, possibly all day tomorrow. We can't afford to wait until you reach La Croix. Now please unbutton your blouse. I promise I won't lose control."

She felt her cheeks heat. "Don't make fun of me."

"I'm perfectly serious."

She didn't know whether to be offended or chagrined. "I'm not accustomed to undressing in public."

"Then you can relax. This is definitely private."

Unconsciously she crossed her arms over her chest, scared, chilled, shivering at what? Being looked at by a man?

Yes. Precisely.

No one had touched her, looked at her since Armand had died, and when he'd been with her, he hadn't been particularly...kind.

Armand had married her to create a political and economic alliance and while the countries had benefited, Chantal had died on the vine.

It was worse than she'd ever imagined. It wasn't the life she thought she'd ever live. She'd been the oldest, the bravest, the surest of herself. She was going to do it all right, make things work for her sisters, her grandparents, for Melio's people. She could do anything, be anything and oh—she'd failed.

She'd been so wrong about everything.

Armand didn't love her. He hadn't even tried to love her. She'd been anything but what he really wanted.

Silly Chantal, silly disillusioned princess living in the tower.

Demetrius's hand settled on the middle of her back, his palm was warm, firm, and it slid up to wrap her shoulder. "Your blouse, Princess. Now."

CHAPTER THREE

THE heat from his hand felt explosive.

Chantal sucked in air, head spinning at the unexpected contact. It'd been so long since anyone touched her. For the past few years there had just been Lilly's arms. Lilly's hugs.

She'd forgotten what a man's hand felt like. Forgotten what even her skin felt like.

His hand lightly gripped her shoulder. Fingers pressed against her upper arm. It wasn't an intimate touch and yet her pulse quickened, blood racing.

Oh God, to be thirty and so lonely...

To be a woman and to not feel anything like a woman.

"Relax." He lightly rubbed her upper arm. "I won't hurt you."

"I know." And she did know. He wasn't the kind of man who'd raise a hand in violence toward a woman. But there was still the other current running through her, the small electric sensation of being touched. Of feeling...real.

His palm slid back up her arm, over her shoulder, covering her collarbone, and then to the upper swell of her breast.

Chantal closed her eyes, held her breath, her body intensely alive. She was both scared and curious.

With her eyes closed, lips parted, she could almost imagine a life she'd never lived. Could see herself someone's wife with a pretty whitewashed house with blue shutters and a view of the sea. She could see the colorful boats tied up at the dock, bobbing happily on the water. She'd hang the laundry outside, sheets and shirts and skirts drying in the sun...

Herbs and cucumbers and tomatoes in the garden. A loaf of crusty bread in the oven. Climbing roses that smelled like musk...

His palm rested on her breast, above her heart. Her pulse raced. Her body flooded with heat. She could feel the hardness of his palm against the softness of her skin.

31

She couldn't move. Couldn't think. Couldn't speak. All her nerves were tuned to the heat of his hand against her body, the feel of his palm on her breast.

"Unbutton your blouse, Princess."

His voice danced across her senses, the no-nonsense Greek inflection riveting. He expected her to obey. He expected her to do exactly as he said.

And yet…and yet…how could that authority, that firmness, that awareness make her feel like this? Something in her responded to his immovable presence, to the maleness, to the fact that he was so different from her.

It made her aware…made her feel…

"Come on, Princess. Or I will."

She trembled, and reached for the first button on her blouse. She couldn't believe she was actually unbuttoning the pink silk blouse. Where was her mind? Where was her will? What was happening to her? How could she be losing control? And yet she didn't stop. Her fingers kept moving. She unbuttoned the delicate blouse until it hung open and then looked at him, muscles tight, nerves wound to the breaking point.

His eyes held hers. He didn't move. He didn't look down at her chest. Instead he stared into her eyes until she felt dizzy and she shuddered, overwhelmed by the strange sensation that she was falling, and yet she couldn't put her hands out, couldn't break her fall.

His hand moved, infinitely slowly, a warm path across her breast, beneath the edge of her blouse to the heated skin below. She jerked at the touch of his skin on hers. The sensation was sharp, hot, and heat curled in her belly, daggerlike fingers of fire.

He heard her hiss. His eyes narrowed. "Does that hurt?"

Yes. No. She struggled to swallow around the lump blocking her throat. "It's…sensitive."

His heavy black brows flattened. But he said nothing. Peeling her blouse back, his gaze dropped, lashes lowering, and he studied her, his gaze taking in her pale skin already darkening with bruises, mottled shades of yellow, green, blue.

"Lean back if you can," he directed. "I'm worried about your ribs."

Goose bumps danced across her skin, the fine hair lifting on her arms, at her nape. His hand made her skin feel so hot, nerves stretched, her body taut, listening as if trying to comprehend what was happening.

What was happening?

What was happening inside her, around her, to the world at large? Chantal felt caught in something so big and chaotic, the dark sky rippling with restless energy, a rumble of thunder and then a deeper growl that stretched from one end of the sky to another.

Her eyes closed as his palm slid across her breast to her shoulder and back again, now slipping along her ribs, beneath the breast, his fingertips gauging the width and span of bone, but this was no impersonal inspection. She felt heat at each pass of his fingers, each stroke across her skin sent little licks of fire, sparks of heat shimmering deeper and deeper into her, sensation burrowing so strong that her womb came to life, all aching emptiness and tension.

No one had made her feel like this in years.

No hand on her breast, no fingers on her hips, no careful exploration of the indentation at her waist. And now this man, this man's hands, this darkness and hot, stormy night everywhere.

Lightning split the sky, wild white fingers of light beyond the edge of the shelter and Chantal shivered.

"Did that hurt?" His mouth was so close to her ear that his deep voice seemed to come from inside her, and she shivered yet again.

"No." Chantal felt almost feverish with heat. His touch was unreal. He was making her feel so much. She'd been alone so long and suddenly his hands, his strength, his close proximity reminded her of everything she'd missed.

Love. Making love. Sex.

Maybe sex was overrated when you were getting it, but take it away, deny it altogether and the body stopped feeling like a real body. Leave the lips just for speech, the hands for tasks, the body just to do essential chores and the life starts to drain away. Bodies have nerves, bodies have skin, bodies contain a spirit, a heart and endless imagination...

His hand settled on her ankle, slowly inspected his way to her knee, and then skimmed her thigh, first outside and then inside and Chantal gasped. Squeezed her eyes. Tried to get control.

"Other leg," he said matter of factly and yet Chantal couldn't stop her pulse from leaping, her belly in knots, her nerves so tense she jumped when his palm circled her left ankle.

"Don't," she choked, knowing she was losing it, losing perspective, losing whatever it was that kept her contained, the iron wall around her emotions. Suddenly she wasn't the fortress of before. She was an open gate and she was begging the forces in.

"Almost done," he said calmly, continuing his examination, ankle, calf, knee—oh knee, her knee was ticklish, all tender nerves and she flinched.

"Not hurt," she whispered breathlessly, willing him to just hurry, just get on with it. If he would finish with this silly med check of his, then she could get back to being the ice princess who needed nothing, no one, not even love.

But he wasn't hurrying. Not in the slightest.

If anything his inspection slowed, his fingertips still resting in the hollow behind her knee, the lightest touch imaginable and yet it sent arrows of feeling up her thighs, between her thighs, feeling that was nearly as intense as the loneliness she never told anyone about.

She wasn't supposed to need.

She wasn't supposed to want.

She wasn't supposed to feel.

Finally, finally his hand wrapped her thigh, moving up, the outer thigh, the back of her hamstring reaching the sensitive skin where thigh met cheek and she jerked so hard that tears rushed to her eyes.

Chantal drew a ragged breath, and then another, completely undone by everything that had happened in the past few hours. She shouldn't be letting him touch her. She shouldn't be responding when he was touching her.

"You're very bruised. You've cracked some ribs. But I think that's the worst of it." His deep voice hurt her ears. Everything about him was making her twist on the inside, her chest, her heart, her emotions so wound up she didn't know how to escape or where to go.

A crooked fork of lightning split the sky just above their heads, and in the stunning bright flash of light, Demetrius's eyes met hers and they were so dark they sank through her, reaching the restless, anxious place where she needed so much and didn't even know how to live with the reality of her life.

He was a man. He was different from her. Altogether different.

"You said you were Greek," she said, conscious of his hand resting on her thigh, near her knee, she dropped her gaze and went to work on the small buttons on her blouse.

"Yes."

Dammit. Her hands were shaking so bad she couldn't even get one button back through the hole. "You live there now?"

"Yes."

"You're in Athens?"

She felt rather than saw him lean toward her. He reached for her blouse. Began to button the silky fabric himself. "I've my own island near Santorini."

He sounded bored, indifferent, but she didn't believe it for one minute. In her experience, Greeks were the proudest of men, the most male. They were passionate, too, and possessive of their women. One of Chantal's college friends had married a member of the Greek aristocracy and she'd been a pampered, and jealously guarded, wife ever since.

Her gaze lifted, she searched his face. His eyes did something to her. They were so dark. So intense. His entire face was hard...fierce. The only softness was at his mouth. There was just a hint of a curve to his lower lip, a suggestion of sexuality that matched the edgy hum in Chantal's veins.

She thought the exam had been difficult. But the matter of fact touch now, the way he buttoned her blouse was worse. She felt so much, needed so much, and the depth of her need appalled her.

Tears filled her eyes again. She clenched her hands at her sides.

"What's wrong?" he demanded gruffly.

She shook her head, afraid to speak. What in God's name was happening to her? Why was she falling apart now?

Thunder boomed, an ear-shattering clap followed immediately by scorching white fingers of light.

"Come here," he said, his gravel accented voice husky, and he dragged her into his arms.

Within the circle of his arms Chantal felt twin rivers of feeling—fear and need.

Hold me.

Let me go.

Want me.

Don't touch me.

His hands reached up, tangled in her hair, tipped her head back. She felt his gaze, a direct piercing look that penetrated all the way through her. "Princesses aren't allowed to cry," he said roughly, and she struggled to smile.

"I know. Rule number one."

"What's rule number two?" He was holding her before him, his hands in her hair trapping her. She couldn't escape his voice, his eyes, his body.

"Not to do anything publicly that would embarrass the family."

"Is that a warning?"

"No. Just a rule."

"And is this public?"

They were in the middle of nowhere, her staff hidden away, back behind the forest with the plane wreckage. "I don't know anymore."

"There's no one here," he said, and his voice was like silk and sandpaper at the same time, sensual, stirring strokes across her senses. "Just us. The sea. The sky."

"And the storm," she added as thunder boomed yet again.

He picked up one of her clenched hands and studied her small fist. "And your fear."

"And my fear," she echoed, her heart beginning to pound harder, heavier.

"Why are you afraid?"

She struggled to swallow, to moisten her mouth, which had

become so dry. Her skin prickled all over. She did feel fear. Tremendous fear. As well as tremendous excitement. "I don't do...this."

"This?" He considered her, a long level gaze. "Why not?"

Her heart pounded so hard she couldn't catch her breath. "It's not allowed."

Demetrius's jaw tightened. Then his head tipped and his mouth covered hers.

Chantal stiffened. For her, all thought stopped, all reaction stilled. She was frozen in endless time. For a long moment she was nowhere, nothing, unable to respond, and then the ice broke, and her mouth trembled, her lips softening beneath his.

She felt his warm breath and the texture of his lips—his mouth both firm and cool. It'd been so long since she kissed anyone she couldn't even remember how she was supposed to do this and yet she couldn't pull away. She needed his touch, this touch, needed the incredible sensation that shot through her, electrifying her.

He kissed her so slowly that she wasn't even sure if they were kissing or touching and her mouth quivered against his, her nerves tightening, her emotions just there, beneath the surface. Her chest contracted, her eyes burned, her breath became more and more shallow. Had she ever felt a kiss like this before? Had she ever been so afraid before?

Chantal reached up to touch his face, uncertain if she was trying to bring him closer or push him away. He was invading her world, ignoring her boundaries. She couldn't let him do this and yet she didn't know how to stop him. It was as if his kiss was life itself. The thunder rolled and boomed, bone shuddering claps overhead and the heat in the air, the humidity of the impending storm, made her want to peel off everything and press herself against him.

"What do I do?" she choked against his mouth. "I don't know what to do..."

"Hush. I do." And lifting her in his arms, he settled her in the sand, her back against the soft grains, the white lightning visible beyond their shelter.

She felt his big, hard body come down on hers, felt the length of his torso, arms, legs. His shoulders covered her, her hips cradled his. She felt as if she'd finally come home.

Demetrius braced his weight on his arms, aware of her fragile ribs, and the pain she'd feel if he allowed her body to support his.

It'd been a long time since he'd been with a woman like this. It wasn't that he'd remained celibate since his wife died, but he hadn't felt something with anyone in so long that feeling anything was stunning. And he wasn't just feeling a little emotion. He was almost overrun by emotion.

They'd been so close to death, and so ready to accept whatever came next, that the relief at returning to life was dazzling. Dizzying.

He felt Chantal's breasts rise and fall, felt her body stir beneath his, her hips lifting, seeking, and lowering his head, he covered her lips once more with his.

He kissed her deeply, kissed with a hunger that words could never explain. Unless you'd been where he'd been, unless you'd seen what he'd seen, unless you knew what he knew, words wouldn't explain the need to merge completely with another, to find release and mindlessness, maybe even an hour of peace.

Peace, he thought, lips parting hers, tongue flicking across the soft, swollen inside of her lip, tasting her mouth and the warmth and wetness within. Peace hadn't been his in years.

Nothing had been his in years.

He'd lost his family, his wife, his circle of friends.

He'd lost it all when he realized he couldn't continue in the Mantheakis tradition, when being a member of his family, his clan, was killing him as surely as it'd killed his wife.

Something had to give.

So he'd given up his past, his future, his soul. But now, here, with the princess, he wasn't quite so disconnected. He felt almost alive again, felt hard and heated and warm. Felt her warmth all the way through him, too.

He'd had sex numerous times in the past few years but he'd never made love.

And somehow, he wanted to make love to the princess who seemed nearly as alone as he was.

His chest burned, hot, hotter, and yet gently he settled his hips against her, even as he kept the brunt of his weight on his arms. He felt her softness shape him, accept him, felt the painful ache of his erection press against her skirt, now hiked high on her thighs.

Her fingers grappled at his shirt, pulling the fabric from his chest. He inhaled sharply as her hand found his bare skin, her fingers seeking skin, muscle, tendon and then he took her tongue in his mouth and sucked the tip of it instead.

She was making him burn. She was making him want. She was making him feel like a young man first falling in love. But this wasn't love. It was fear. It was exhilaration. It was gratitude for making it through another day.

Her fingertips brushed his nipple and he stifled a groan. Her touch unsettled him, light, searching and yet edged with desperation as if she too knew it was this one moment, and only this moment, that whatever was happening would never happen again.

If that were the case, he'd hold her, fill her, give her all that he'd withheld from the women who'd entered and disappeared from his life in the years since Katina died.

With her assistance, his shirt came off. His slacks were next. The underclothes disappeared from them both and when he lay her down again they were both completely naked and their skin felt so right that way, one body close to the other.

He felt the princess draw a quick breath as his hand caressed her hip, shaping her curves. She was so slender, delicate, and he urged her closer yet, her shoulder brushing against his, her soft breasts pressed to his chest.

He briefly shifted his weight, settled between her legs and immediately felt his body seek for hers, searching for her warmth, her heat, and he felt the softness of her against him, felt the way her body gave.

This was madness, he knew, this wasn't why he'd agreed to protect her. This wasn't part of any job description he'd ever known, but he couldn't stop. Not now. Not today. Not when the thunder boomed and the lightning crackled and their bodies and skin was the only thing keeping them sane.

Reaching between their bodies he lightly touched Chantal's smooth flat belly, cupped her mound, slipped his hand between her legs to feel if she was ready for him, and she was. Her body was warm, wet, willing. Was this right? he wondered, even as he kissed her more deeply. How could making love be an answer to anything?

And yet her body felt wonderful, and her warmth called to him, drawing something in him that he'd refused to recognize in years.

She wasn't just a body, but a woman, a woman with a life that had been as challenging as his.

And when he entered her, slowly easing into her, pushing as deep as he could go without hurting her, he felt something inside him split, a small tear, and he knew then, that he'd made a huge tactical error. This wasn't a woman he could have. But she wasn't a woman he could forget, either.

The storm was over. It had to be morning, but Chantal didn't want to open her eyes. She didn't want to wake up until Demetrius was gone. But Demetrius wasn't moving. He was lying right next to her, his body curved around hers, his hand resting on her bare hip.

She'd spent the night in his arms. All night in his arms. The lovemaking had been intense, explosive, almost frightening in its carnal volatility. They could have been animals instead of people, two starving human beings.

But she *had* been starving. Starving for years.

Shuddering at the image, Chantal opened her eyes, her heavy lashes fluttering up to face the clear pale blue sky, the morning light the sheerest shade of gold, the air still and warm, the only sound that of the crash of waves on the beach.

Pushing up on her elbow, she winced at the stab of pain and combed her hair back from her face as she tried to stay calm.

This wasn't something she should have done. This wasn't something she could condone. Frantic grapplings in the dark were reserved for teenagers randy with hormones, not a middle-aged woman with a young child.

Swallowing the icy lump in her throat, hating how it matched the even heavier icy rock in her stomach, she slowly rolled out from beneath his hand, biting a groan of anguish at the sharp pain stabbing deep in her ribs, spreading into her chest, radiating through the middle of her back.

My God, she hurt. But she forced herself to her feet, and stepped over the scattered palm fronds. The storm had blown their little shelter to bits, and the high ocean tide had practically swept them out to sea.

Not that the storm, or the tide, had stopped them last night. Nothing had stopped them. Not even dignity, pride, or common sense.

Limping along the beach, Chantal searched for her missing clothing, and tried to pretend she wasn't stark naked.

This had to be someone else's life. This couldn't be her, this couldn't have been her horrible nightmare.

She'd had sex with a stranger.

Not just once, but two, three times.

Cringing, she turned, scanned the sea, saw nothing beyond the beautiful beach, so peaceful now, the sand swept clean by rain and sea, and then glanced back at Demetrius who still slept.

Who the hell was he? She knew nothing about him. Absolutely nothing. He could be a reporter. A friend of her father-in-law's. He could be married. He could be infectious.

Chantal froze, her insides cramping.

She could get pregnant.

They'd had unprotected sex. Three times. She could definitely get pregnant.

Panic rose, a wide wave of panic even stronger than last night's high tide. She pressed her hands to her eyes, blocked out the vision of what they'd done, what they'd been to each other then, and tried to focus on facts. On reality.

She'd never been highly fertile—she and Armand had had a year of unprotected sex before she conceived Lilly—and she shouldn't be in that part of her cycle, anyway.

Besides, lots of people had unprotected sex and they didn't get pregnant. The timing had to be next to impossible. The chances, the odds…

What was done, was done, she sharply reminded herself. Don't get hysterical. Just get your clothes. Get dressed. Get out of here.

She searched for her blouse, her skirt, and spotted them on the beach, wet, bedraggled, soggy with saltwater and sand. The surf must have carried them out and then brought them back again. Sighing, she hurried across the unscarred sand for her things. The clothes were chilly, damp and gritty but Chantal dragged the blouse on anyway and stepped into the short skirt, the pale pink silk fabric now stained a dappled purple gray.

What a waste of a couture suit.

Sick at heart, Chantal turned slowly, away from the ocean with the fingers of white foam to the long sandy expanse behind her and froze. Demetrius was awake, and watching her.

He was half-sitting, propped on one elbow. His expression was closed, guarded. What on earth was he thinking? But no, actually, she didn't want to know what he was thinking right now. She didn't want to have any part of him. What she wanted was to run—get as far away from him as possible but there was nowhere to go—at least not yet.

Slowly, deliberately, she headed toward him, trying to ignore that the cold wet blouse clung to her bare breasts, that her soaked skirt hugged her hips like shrink-wrapped cellophane, and her undergarments were probably floating out at sea.

Yet on reaching his side she saw her crumpled petal-pink lace bra and matching pink panties bunched in his hand.

Chantal's eyes burned. Her stomach hurt. Her pride felt battered. "Please," she said, putting out her hand in an imperial gesture.

Silently he handed her the delicate under wire bra and lace panties.

"Thank you," she gritted, tears of shame scalding her eyes.

"My pleasure." His eyes glowed at her, a warning in the dark depths. "Princess."

CHAPTER FOUR

DEMETRIUS was angry. Ridiculously angry. He had no right to be angry, either.

He knew last night was a one-time only, he knew when he woke this morning that he'd never let his control slip like that again, and yet the knowledge did nothing to ease the hot, livid emotion building inside him.

The fact that he still had any emotion inside him shocked him.

He'd been the vigilante—the terminator—so long he hadn't thought he could care about people, needs, *feelings*. But he was caring about something at the moment, and it was a mistake. Emotions got in the way of him doing his job.

"How are the ribs?" he asked, his voice coming out short, curt. He shouldn't still be sitting here naked. He shouldn't still be fighting desire. He shouldn't even be thinking about stripping the still damp skirt and blouse off her curvy body and putting his mouth against her sun warmed skin and drinking her like a sweet strawberry Italian soda.

His body hardened. It was impossible to forget how she'd felt beneath him. He was ready to take her again, ready to slide his hands across her breasts, her belly, her thighs. Ready to feel her squirm and whimper and cry with pleasure.

"Fine," she answered crisply, balling her undergarments tighter into her hand.

He felt his lips twist in a savage smile. Last night she'd been broken...open...but this morning she'd remembered who she was, who he was, what her title represented. Princess Chantal Marie Thibaudet, born Princess Chantal Marie Ducasse, probably the world's most beautiful, famous princess. No one was more photographed. No one was more regal.

And she was regal now, even with her long dark hair loose over her shoulders. Even with the wet clothes clinging to her slender figure, she managed to tip her straight nose, press her

43

full mouth tight. She'd become so perfectly proper again. She'd become exactly who she was supposed to be and even though it was right, it made his head hurt, his pulse pound, made him want to lose his temper as only he could lose his temper.

And he had one hell of a temper, too.

"Do you mind turning around?" she said icily, gesturing with her finger.

He ground his teeth together. Did she honestly think he hadn't seen everything? That he hadn't memorized every curve of her body, every dip and hollow and soft satin place?

But she was staring at him, pointedly, and with an exasperated sigh he rose.

Chantal's heart stuttered and then nearly broke through her chest as Demetrius slowly got to his feet.

How she could have fallen so willingly into his arms?

He was huge. Muscular. Intimidating. Armand had been an aristocrat, medium height, lithe, slender, with hands like a pianist—long slender fingers, narrow wrists. Demetrius Mantheakis was anything but narrow and slender. He was thickly built, broad through the shoulder, deep in the chest, thighs, butt hard with tight, compact muscle. Dark hair shadowed his chest, formed a fine trail down his flat, carved abdomen to a thatch at his thighs. Male, his body screamed, I am all male.

She wanted to avert her eyes but knew it was too late. They'd been...intimate. Very. Besides, she'd been married before, conceived a child, delivered a child. It wasn't as if she didn't know how men's bodies worked, how men and women came together for pleasure and procreation.

But their joining last night had had nothing to do with procreation, which left just pleasure.

With his back to her, she struggled out of her blouse again, groaning softly at the effort of trying to hook the bra. Each lift of her arm, each twist lanced pain through her, hot and sharp. Blinking back tears, she tried to get the hook to take a second time.

"Enough," Demetrius ground out, turning around. He took the delicate straps of the bra from her and deftly hooked the bra closed. "It's absurd to not let me help you."

''I don't want your help.''

''Too bad, isn't it?'' He bent down, picked up her blouse from her feet and held it out.

''You shouldn't—'' she broke off, bit hard on the inside of her cheek, held the recriminations in. She couldn't blame him. She'd allowed it to happen.

Worse, she'd *wanted* it to happen.

He buttoned the blouse for her, even tucked it into the waistband of her skirt, and heat filled her at the brush of his fingers against her skin. Eyes closed, she felt her stomach clench and remembered the way his body had joined with hers, how his body had taken hers, a deep, relentless assault on her frozen self.

How to stay cold when someone so hot, so hard was taking your breath away? He'd filled her completely, driven every thought from her mind until all she felt, all she wanted, all she needed was him. Each thrust of his hips rocked her world, creating wave after wave of excruciating sensation. She couldn't survive pleasure like that. It'd been so intense, too intense, and yet he wouldn't let her hold back. He just kept driving into her, hard, thick thrusts that sent her shattering.

''Thank you,'' she said stiffly as he finished his task and took a step away. And she commended herself for sounding so cool when on the inside she felt feverish all over again. She had to forget. She had to put the memory of her shuddering response out of mind. Had to block out how she'd held onto him for ages, her body rippling with aftershock after aftershock, her nails pressed to his shoulders. Had to forget that he'd just about finished her off when he kissed her breast, suckling her aching nipple.

How did some men know exactly what to do? How could Armand, with all his experience, never give her any pleasure? How could lying with Demetrius here on the beach become the most sexual, sensual night of her life?

''What about the panties?'' he drawled.

She went hot, cold, and she fought to keep her gaze above his waist. He was so powerfully made, and with his magnificent body completely naked, she discovered he was hard, very hard. She found his arousal this morning shocking and exciting. What did *he* think of last night? Was it good for him, or had it all been about her?

His dark eyes met hers and held.

She felt a shiver race up and down her back. In the morning light he looked even more dominant than he did at night. While the storm had raged, he'd held her safe in his arms and now she knew why. Demetrius wasn't about to be blown away by sea breezes or tropical storms. He wasn't about to be blown away by anything.

"I can help you," he reminded her.

"Please." She meant to sound sarcastic, instead it came out breathless. She was losing control again, and she knew she couldn't. "This was a mistake, Mr. Mantheakis——"

"I think we're past formalities now, Chantal."

The way he said her name sent another hot shiver racing through her, flashes of feeling in her belly. She was burning hot on the inside. "Could you please put some clothes on?"

He smiled. Grimly. "Of course, Princess."

Relations were most definitely strained, Chantal thought, disgusted with herself. He'd been wonderful on the plane, the kind of man she might have actually enjoyed as a friend, but now...now...

Never.

"What exactly do you do?" she asked, digging into the sand with a little stick, trying to ignore the growling of her stomach, the heat around them, the near sweltering conditions. According to her watch, it was close to noon and he still refused to let her return to the plane wreckage—something she found utterly absurd—but at this point, with tender ribs and a stunning headache, she wasn't going to test him.

"I have my own business."

She tried to imagine what kind of business he'd be in. "You're successful?"

"Very."

She nodded and poked the stick deeper into the hole she'd dug, finding water down below the surface sand. "And you have your own island?"

"Yes."

Chantal heard a droning sound overhead, a faraway hum of engine. "Do you hear that?" she asked, tilting her head back, scanning the endlessly blue sky. She didn't wait for Demetrius to answer. She struggled to her feet, pressing her right arm to her side to keep the tender ribs and surrounding muscles as still as possible.

Suddenly a plane swooped low overhead from behind the tall trees of the rainforest. Chantal let out a shout of relief. "They found us!"

The plane circled the island. It descended even lower, making a final approach. "We should go. It's landing," she said, checking the buttons on her blouse, then the hem of her salt-stained skirt.

Demetrius didn't move. "That's not our plane."

"It's a rescue plane." She was hot and hungry and ready for a shower and clean clothes. And if he wasn't going to head back, fine, but she wasn't about to waste another minute here. "Fine. Stay here. I don't care."

He reached out, circled her ankle, held her still. "It's not our plane," he repeated.

She very nearly kicked his hand, his fingers so warm, too warm against her bare skin. "Let go."

"Once you sit down."

This wasn't even about power. It was survival, pure and simple. Demetrius Mantheakis was too much for her. She couldn't handle him, couldn't even handle herself around him. "I don't want to sit down. I want to go join my staff. I want to board the plane—"

"We're waiting for a different plane, Princess."

She could feel his fingers wrap around each of the small bones in her ankle, feel his warm firm palm along the back of her anklebone and she shivered. His fingers tightened.

"I don't think you understand me, Demetrius. I don't want to wait for another plane. I want this one."

"I'm sorry."

She yanked on her ankle, got nowhere at all. "*Stop*. Just stop this game right now. I want to go."

"You can't."

She felt a shaft of cold, her skin prickling with heightened nerves. "You're beginning to frighten me."

"I've no desire to frighten you. It's my job to protect you." He released her, fluidly stood. "Your safety is my number one concern."

She stared at him for the longest moment, eyes searching the hard planes of his face, the dark stubble on his square jaw. "Why? What do you mean?"

"You've no idea who I am, do you?"

She hated the confusion filling her, and her lips pressed, her heart beating double fast. "No." There was much more she wanted to say but she'd learned years ago to ask only the most pressing questions, to fight only the most essential battles. But surely, this was one of those battles. "Who are you?"

His eyes creased at the corners. He looked as if he were enjoying a private joke. "Your shadow."

She might have learned to bite her tongue, but Chantal hated sarcasm and cryptic answers. It was so typical of the kind of answers Armand and his people gave her, answers indicating that she didn't need to know certain things, answer indicating that as a woman she ought to be ignored...lied to.

Her nails dug into her palms. She'd had it with the lies, had it with the silence. "My shadow? As in—" her eyes searched his, trying to see past the hard veneer that hid his thoughts and all his emotions "—bodyguard?"

"Exactly."

She frowned, increasingly uncomfortable. Maybe she'd never handpicked her security detail, but she'd always been part of the final selection process and been promptly introduced to new staff. "I didn't hire you."

"No."

She felt a muscle twitch between her eyebrows, a small convulsive tug. "Then...?"

He gave her a long, level look, as if weighing what he could tell her, weighing what he would tell her. It was already clear to her that he wasn't accustomed to confiding in women. But then, she wasn't an ordinary woman, either. "Your brother-in-law, King Nuri, hired me—"

"Malik?"

"—With your grandfather's blessing."

Chantal felt cold despite the simmering heat. She reached up, blotted her forehead with the back of her hand. Her skin was beaded, damp, and yet she felt chilly on the inside. "I'm afraid the heat is getting to me. I don't understand. Nothing you're saying is making sense—"

"You're not listening, then."

She needed a bath. Sand and sea coated her skin. The heat and humidity wasn't helping, either. "Then say it again."

"Your family hired me to protect you."

"Why?"

"You're in danger."

No. She wasn't. How absurd. "Somebody would have said something to me. My sister...my grandfather."

"I've been shadowing you two weeks, Princess."

Her head snapped back. She stared at him appalled. "Two weeks?"

"Everywhere you've been, I've been."

"The fashion shows?"

"The receptions and cocktail parties."

A world shimmered precariously beyond her reach, a whole world rotating on an axis and she could see it, imagine it, but she wasn't part of it. "The breakfast at the hotel?"

"I know exactly the waiter you were talking about. She was my waiter, too."

Chantal noticed that Demetrius had referred to the waiter as she. Demetrius understood the waiter's need to be someone else, too. Somehow the thought settled her, calmed her. She focused her thoughts, forced herself to regroup. "Why do you think I'm in danger?"

But before he could answer there was a loud humming noise and the humming turned into a full roar. The jet that had landed fifteen minutes ago was taking off.

For a long moment she stared at the belly of the white glossy jet, watching the wheels, the tilt of the aircraft's nose.

Then panic hit and she screamed. "No. No. Not without me!"

She chased after the plane, running barefoot along the beach, blindly kicking up saltwater and sand.

But the jet kept rising and the wheels folded, disappeared. Tears filled her eyes as the jet sailed off, away from the island into the endless blue sky.

She dropped to her knees, tears of hurt and rage filling her eyes. She wanted to go home. She needed to go home. She'd never been away from Lilly for more than a week. Seven days. That was her limit. She'd made it clear from the beginning that she'd fulfill her royal duties, but when scheduling her appointments the staff had to accept that no matter the occasion, no matter the reason, she'd never leave her daughter for longer than a week.

She should have been home last night. Which made today day eight.

"My jet will be landing shortly."

She hadn't heard Demetrius approach and she shook her head, hating him, hating him for keeping her away from her daughter. "I wanted to be on that plane. I wanted to go home. Now. Today." She reached up and wiped away her tears, feeling overwrought. "You have no idea how much I miss Lilly."

Demetrius stared down on Chantal's dark hair, the long strands blowing in the gentle breeze. The first clouds were appearing on the horizon. True to the tropics, the wind would pick up, rain clouds would gather, there'd be another spectacular storm later.

She was wrong about one thing, he thought, watching the breeze lift and blow her hair. He understood how much she missed her daughter. He'd lost his wife and child. And he'd never stopped longing to see them, touch them, hold them just once more.

He'd made endless bargains with God, promised his heart, his home, his soul if Katina and their daughter could be spared.

God, he learned, didn't bargain.

"I miss her," Chantal repeated softly, tipping her head back to watch the jet—now just a speck in the sky—disappear from sight.

"And she'll miss you, but better we keep you safe."

"So when does your plane arrive?" She asked, unable to keep her voice from breaking.

"Soon."

"And your plane will fly me to La Croix?"

He was silent a long moment. "We're not going back to La Croix."

Chantal was glad she was sitting. Her bones felt dangerously weak. "Not going home?"

He took a step toward her and then another, until his body dwarfed hers, his shadow stretching long, a tower of a man. "Not immediately."

"My daughter's in La Croix," Chantal said quietly, firmly, grateful she'd spent years learning the art of camouflage.

"I know. But we're not going there."

"Where are we going then?"

"To the Rock."

"The Rock?"

"My island."

Chantal fought down her anguish. "And Lilly?"

"She'll be safe in La Croix with your family."

Armand's family. Chantal averted her head, faced the ocean, watched the waves, which were beginning to turn dark green beneath the early-afternoon clouds. A storm was moving in. Again. She suppressed a shiver. She didn't want to be here when the next storm hit. Didn't think she could survive being caught in the middle of another storm with Demetrius Mantheakis. He was a storm in and of itself. "My daughter should be with me."

"She will be."

"They won't let her leave the country." She spoke carefully, finding it painful to speak difficult truths out loud. "Part of my…contract…as princess is that I can leave, but Lilly, who shall inherit the throne must stay behind." She felt the lump block and fill her throat, cutting off air, making her head swim. "She's La Croix's only heir."

"Then for now she remains with her father's family."

The Greek's voice sounded flinty, almost indifferent and Chantal bowed her head, hiding her pain. "I need her." She could barely squeeze the words out. It was nearly impossible for

her to claim what she needed most. And she needed her daughter.
Her daughter had been everything for her so long...her daughter
had been her sole reason for living, breathing, her daughter was
life itself.

"You'll be with her again." He crouched in front of her,
forced her chin up, stared long and hard into her eyes. "Even-
tually. Once it's safe. For you, and her."

Chantal swallowed around the hot pain filling her, a lance
through her heart. "You don't believe she's in danger, do you?"

"No. But you definitely are."

She flinched, but it wasn't his words, which frightened her, it
was him. She realized the others were gone. She realized they
were alone, truly alone together, and the situation terrified her.
Him, her, alone. Him, her... "And once we're on your island...?"

"I'll be able to keep you safe my way."

She hesitated, unbalanced. "*Your* way?"

"My people, my island, my control."

He called this an island? Chantal asked herself, leaning sideways
in her seat to see the land loom up below them.

Greek islands were supposed to be beautiful. This was a piece
of black rock in the middle of the sea.

Moments later the jet touched down on the shortest runway
imaginable, and the moment they deplaned they were traveling
in a dark Mercedes convertible with Demetrius at the wheel.

Still wearing her stained silk suit, Chantal pressed her hands
to the side of her seat, her nerves absolutely shot.

During the flight, they'd had a hot meal and slept, but
Demetrius had spoken very little.

But now, driving, he glanced at her, and finally she registered
on his personal radar screen. "We're almost at the house," he
said.

She couldn't imagine how anyone could live on such a barren
black rock. "A real house?"

"With indoor plumbing." Rare amusement lurked at the corner of his mouth.

But she wasn't amused. The last thing she felt like doing was
laughing.

"So when can I call my daughter?"

The amusement faded from his expression. "You can't."

He couldn't keep her from phoning her own family. He didn't have that kind of power. "You forget, Demetrius, you work for me."

"Actually, Princess, I work for the sultan."

She chafed at the way he said, *princess,* resenting his authority and the mockery she heard in his voice. "He's not going to approve of how you're treating me."

"He knows my methods."

"I wouldn't be so sure of that," she flashed, pressing her fists to her thighs, trying desperately hard to hang on to the last scraps of her royal dignity. Somehow he'd managed to strip her of everything else.

"And so do my people," he added, shooting her a warning glance. "Don't think they'll loan you a phone, a boat, or a plane."

"*Your* people?"

His head, with the thick jet-black hair, inclined. "The Rock is my world. Everything on this island is part of that world, and it's the only world I trust. Those that live here, work here, work for me."

"Are you sure you don't own them?" she flashed, provoked beyond reason, remembering her years in La Croix. Armand had acted like he owned her and she'd hated it.

But Demetrius wasn't perturbed. He looked at her, shrugged. "Of course not. They're not objects to possess. But I own their loyalty. They are my people."

She stared at his profile now, questions racing through her head, making the short drive from airport to house interminable. How did she know she could trust him? How did she know anything he said was true? It was quite possible he was the threat.

Emotion coiled inside her, tighter, tighter until she felt like a child's wood top about to spring loose.

What if, just what if, he really hadn't been hired by Nicolette's sultan? What if he worked for someone else? What if...?

She shot him another suspicious glance, unsettled by the high bridge of his nose, the hard prominent cheekbones. The lines in his face were so dominant, so strong. She'd never known another man with a face that looked as if it'd been gouged from stone.

"If there's something on your mind," he said flatly, his gaze never leaving the narrow twisting mountain road, "say it."

Say it? She silently wondered, thinking of the past. The problem was she'd spent too many years silent, biting her tongue, holding back her protests. She didn't know how to say what she needed to say, didn't know the words...

There'd been years and years of being politely ignored. Years where the attention was focused on the man—the male definition of experience. In La Croix she'd never been a woman, not a real person, much less a royal princess. She'd simply been a companion. It was as if each tour, each visit, each appearance was strictly for Armand's benefit. She was only seen when she was at his side.

His side. *His* pleasure. *His* interest.

Now and then guides and interpreters would engage her in conversation when she was alone, on her own, waiting. But the moment Armand appeared, all friendliness vanished. Silence fell. Energy, attention focused exclusively on Armand.

She'd had no idea how strong her feelings were until she wasn't allowed to express them. Armand's culture was the culture of men. It wasn't merely arrogant—it was oblivious to the feminine. For most La Croix men, a woman was to be seen, not heard, to be beautiful, but pliable, to comply, compromise, acquiesce.

Acquiesce.

She'd spent her life giving herself up, giving herself out, giving, giving, would there ever be time for herself? Room for herself? How was a woman supposed to survive in a world like this?

"I can't answer your fears if you don't tell me what's worrying you—"

"I'm not afraid."

"And I can't help you, if you don't tell me what you need," he continued as if she hadn't spoken.

Help her? How could he possibly help her? He was a man. Anger surged through her and balling her hands into fists, she held the fury in.

Suddenly she pictured herself standing on the top of Demetrius's mountain and screaming up into the sky, screaming at the stars and the sun and the dawn, screaming at the night. *Look at me. See me. I am real, aren't I? I must matter, don't I?*

I matter.

I do.

"We're here," Demetrius said abruptly, parking in front of a tall whitewashed house, stark, simple.

The air caught in her throat. She'd never seen such a severe looking house in her life. How could he live here? The building looked as cold and hard as a hospital.

Or a prison.

Demetrius turned off the engine. "Welcome to your new home."

CHAPTER FIVE

"THIS isn't my home," Chantal said fiercely, still sitting in the Mercedes convertible, her gaze fixed on the large white plaster house, the no-nonsense windows, the intensely blue sky behind the barely visible terra cotta tiled roof. Even the stairs wrapping the side of the house were boxy, rectangular, all straight white lines and angles.

He stopped on the front steps and faced her. "For the next month it is."

Month? Was he out of his mind? She struggled to scramble from the convertible, her right side tightening with red-hot pain as she pushed open the car door. Her ribs had been on fire ever since they boarded the plane but the physical pain was nothing compared to the loss of Lilly. "You don't actually mean a *month.*"

His dark narrowed glance swept over her face with its furrowed brow and compressed lips. He shook his head once, a short, impatient shake of his head. "You're in no condition to fight with me. You can hardly stand up straight."

Was that a challenge? Ignoring the intense throbbing between her ribs, Chantal forced her shoulders back. "I'm fine."

He gestured dismissively, indicating her paleness, the pinched muscles at her mouth. "I'll let the doctor be the judge of that. He's on his way."

Inside the house, Demetrius climbed the stairs to his second floor bedroom suite, checking messages on his cell phone's voice mail at the same time.

Most calls weren't urgent, but the message from palace security in Melio was. He called the chief of security as he walked to his bedroom window that overlooked the front driveway. The princess was still leaning against the hood of his car. She looked furious. Frustrated.

He didn't exactly blame her. He was damn frustrated, too. Sex

56

had been a mistake. He should have never lost control. But blame would do nothing now. The mistake had been made, and he'd learned long ago that once history was written, you couldn't go back and rewrite it.

Those first couple years after he made the break with his family—*The* Family—he expected a bullet in his back any day. You didn't leave the family. He'd been the first in decades. But his anger had been so huge, his loss so severe, that somehow the different warring sides respected his pain, accepted their part in the tragedy, and they let him go.

Of course there had been attempts to bring him back 'home', attempts to influence him—persuade—money, psychological intimidation, physical threats, but Demetrius was far too angry, emotions far too numb, to fear death. So he got life. And he had his revenge and he carved out his freedom for himself, one job at a time.

The vigilante had become the professional, the expert on solving crime, predicting crime, protecting from crime.

Now his security firm was considered one of the best in the world, if not the best, and he'd made a fortune off people's fear, built an empire on the notion that what happened to Katina should never happen to anyone else.

"Demetrius? Still there?" Avel Dragonouis, the Greek security expert Demetrius had sent to Melio to work with the palace detectives came on the line. "Sorry to keep you waiting."

"What's happened?"

"There was a camera in her room at the palace here," Avel said bluntly. "We found it patched into a wall. It's not particularly hi-tech, can't be police or government equipment, either. This is your typical consumer video camera."

Demetrius felt his gut tighten. "Where was the camera?"

"Positioned over her bed."

A Peeping Tom pervert, too. "Has anyone checked her rooms in La Croix?"

"So far the king and queen have refused to cooperate in our investigation—"

"We just want her room checked," Demetrius interrupted bitterly, exasperated by Princess Chantal's inflexible, in-laws.

"They feel it's an invasion of privacy."

"Better to lose the princess, right?" Demetrius sighed, rubbed his forehead. "Fine. Keep me posted."

Hanging up, Demetrius glanced out the window again, saw Chantal nervously rub her hands against the car's glossy paint.

Her head was bent. Her face concealed. And yet he felt her vulnerability keenly. Her royal family, the Ducasses, were worried sick about her, and yet in La Croix, the Thibaudets couldn't be bothered.

The Thibaudets needed investigating.

Before stepping into the shower, Demetrius made one more call, this time to his Athens office. It was time a serious inquiry was launched into Phillipe and Catherine Thibaudets' lives. Demetrius wanted to know everything about them. He also wanted to know everything possible about Armand, their late son, their only child, the prince Chantal had married.

No detail was too small, Demetrius told his Athens assistant. No detail irrelevant.

In the shower Demetrius reflected on everything he knew about Chantal. Her American mother. The idyllic childhood in Melio. The loss of her parents at fourteen. Her protective relationship with her sisters. Her difficult marriage. Her young daughter. Her pride.

And it was her pride that jeopardized her most.

The princess didn't know when to ask for help. The Princess didn't know how to ask for help.

He was right to bring her to the Rock. The Rock was the ultimate refuge, the island was off-limits to everyone. No one arrived by boat, plane, or helicopter without his permission. The few families living and working here had been with him for years, most were people he'd saved in one way or another, and for those rescued from the sure hand of death, life on the Rock was secure and sweet.

People here knew exactly who he was, and exactly what he did, and they were grateful he didn't pull any punches.

Dressing in khaki-colored linen slacks and a black knit short-sleeve shirt he ran his fingers through his short dark hair and returned down the stairs to discover the princess had entered the house and was wandering through the lower floor.

Chantal passed through virtually empty rooms, the interior of the house as Spartan as the outside. As she moved from one room to the next, the whitewashed walls remained empty, the furniture low and sparse, no decoration anywhere. No pictures, no books, no television, nothing for entertainment or pleasure.

And suddenly he was there, appearing so silently in the doorway, that she felt a shudder deep inside her. He terrified her. Not because he'd ever hurt her, but because he'd made her feel so much on Sao Tome, the island the plane had landed on. He'd made her want so much again.

Briefly her gaze met his before she looked away, heat creeping through her face, burning her. "Your house is empty," she said, nerves strung tight, body humming with a restless energy she couldn't explain.

"I have what I need."

Even without looking at him, she felt the way he studied her, assessed her. He was an expert in observation. "So what do you do here?" she asked, trying to fill the peculiar quiet. "How do you pass the time?"

"I work."

"You have an office here then?"

"Downstairs."

He hadn't moved from the doorway. He was so big he filled the opening in the white plastered walls and the light pouring through the open window lit his face, clear defining light accenting the broad jaw and brow.

"You've been a bodyguard for a while now?" she asked, picking through the dozens of questions and doubts filling her brain.

"Awhile."

He wasn't giving her much to work with, was he? "You don't look like a bodyguard."

"Do they come in a standard package?"

"I've had bodyguards before."

"Were they any good?"

She shrugged. "I'm still here, aren't I?"

He said nothing and his silence set loose a fresh flurry of

worries and doubts inside of her. She didn't know how to deal with him. Didn't know how to distance herself, either. He was inconsequential, she told herself. He didn't matter. He had no impact on her life.

But that wasn't true.

He'd rocked her world with his body, and then rocked it again when he'd told her she was in his protection.

Protection. The word was supposed to evoke safety. Comfort. Peace. But she felt anything but safe, comfortable or peaceful right now. "Is this where you bring all your clients?" She blurted, panic growing. How could she spend a month here? How could she spend a month with *him?*

"You're the first."

"And the lack of neighbors?"

"I like my privacy."

"Do you even have phones?"

"Yes, but I have a security code on them. No one can use them without me dialing the code first."

Chantal felt precariously close to tears. She needed a bath, a change of clothes, a good nap. But most of all, she needed to find a touchstone, something familiar, something from home to reassure her. Settle her. "Can I at least call Lilly?"

"No. You're too emotional."

Because I'm scared! She ground her teeth together, fighting her anger, the waves of indignation. "What about making a call to my sister, Nicollette? Or to my grandfather?"

He shook his head. "There's no point. They know what they need to know—the plane crashed, there were frightening moments, but you're now safe with me."

Safe with him? Chantal nearly choked on the tears she was holding inside. Nothing about Demetrius was safe—much less her own person. She'd stripped for him, opened her body for him, nearly opened her heart for him. How could this...*he*...be considered safe?

"I realize you've been hired to protect me," she said tersely, speaking flatly, precisely, empowered by the oldest survival skill of all time: self-preservation. She'd never make it here, not alone with him. "But I won't be kept isolated from my home and my family this way. Perhaps you enjoy your isolation here on the Rock, but I need my family. I need to be with them. And I need to go home—''

''Even if it kills you?'' He interrupted, folding his arms, causing the shirt to gape.

''An exaggeration,'' she said, trying to avoid looking at his bronze throat and the dense muscle of his chest. She remembered what it felt like to lie against that chest, to have his warm, powerful body arched above hers, hips tight, legs tangled. He made love the way some made war—accepting nothing less than complete and total surrender.

And she'd loved it. Perhaps that's what humiliated her most. She hadn't merely accepted him, she'd wanted him desperately. She'd been completely wanton, craving everything he gave her and more.

He'd been so big inside her, so hard, so hot, and even after he'd come, she hadn't wanted him to withdraw from her. She'd loved the feel of him too much, loved the way their bodies had fit together. There'd been no thought, no control on her part.

She'd dug her nails into his back trying to hold him tighter, trying to merge even closer.

Insatiable, she thought now, ashamed all over again. She couldn't get enough, and he knew it.

Heat flooded her body, mindless heat, her legs trembling a little, her muscles inside her belly clenching.

''When was the last time the Thibaudets visited the palace in Melio?'' he asked abruptly.

She eyed him warily. ''Six months or so. They flew to Melio for Nicolette's wedding to King Nuri.''

''Did anyone else from La Croix come?''

Her shoulders twisted. ''Plenty. Both the king and queen have brothers and sisters as well as cousins. Why?''

''Someone close to you, someone with access to you wants you…gone.''

Gone? Gone as in *dead?* She blanched but held her ground, those years of training coming in handy as she struggled to mask the depth of her shock.

''There've been two attempts that we know of,'' he continued in the same hard, uncompromising voice, his Greek accent more pronounced then it had been last night. "The first attempt was foiled purely by chance. The second was nearly fatal."

"I don't..." She swallowed, feeling sick on the inside, nausea and ice somersaulting in her veins. "I don't know anything about an attempt, and certainly nothing about one being nearly fatal."

"You were sick after your sister's wedding." His deep voice forced her to meet his gaze again.

"I had the flu."

"You were hospitalized."

"For a day."

"Two days."

"Dehydration."

"Blood work was done." He moved toward her, touched the base of her neck, his fingertip brushing the hollow of her throat.

She jerked at the touch, her pulse leaping wildly. His touch was hot and sharp, both delicious and disconcerting.

"You were being poisoned," he continued ruthlessly.

"No."

"Your doctor in La Croix alerted the king and queen—"

His words and touch made her head spin, and Chantal glanced right, left, unable to take in what he was saying. It couldn't be true. There was no reason for him to lie to her...and yet, what did she know of him? Who was he? A man. And she knew perfectly well that men had agendas of their own. "I never heard anything about it," she said hoarsely.

"Of course not." The corner of his mouth lifted but he looked harsh, angry, as though he were barely hanging onto his temper. "The good doctor was forbidden to speak of it to you. He was told that you'd done it to yourself, that you'd turned increasingly self-destructive since your husband's death and this was just another attention seeking behavior."

"What?"

Even more slowly Demetrius ran a finger up the side of her throat. "A cry for help," he concluded, and she shivered even as tendrils of heat curled in her belly, re-igniting the fire, turning her into a mass of trembling nerves.

Just like last night his touch scorched her and the need had returned, resurrecting the memory of pleasure. The pleasure had been stunning. Nothing had ever compared to the earthy, sensuality in her life. No one had ever touched her as if she was both beautiful and real, and it felt incredible to love her body, her skin, her mind.

Her mind...

Her mind had always been her greatest strength. Her reason. Her discipline. Her tremendous drive. And yet he was telling her now that the king and queen didn't think she was mentally sound. Worse, they'd actually told her physician that she'd apparently poisoned herself to get attention.

How repulsive. As if she'd ever hurt herself when she had so much to live for! "That's ridiculous," she choked, stepping away, senses spinning, nerves stretched taut. She had to put distance between them before her body betrayed her again. Her mind was strong. It was her body that was weak. "I might have issues with my in-laws, but I've no desire to leave this life."

"And I've no desire to see you leave this life, either."

"Who poisoned me, then?"

"If we knew, I wouldn't have you in protective custody."

Protective custody. What a horrible phrase. She turned, glanced back at him. "Any ideas? Possible leads?"

"The Melio palace security is taking the lead in the investigation. Of course my staff is working with them, but our primary job is to keep you safe, not solve the crime." He hesitated. "But at the moment we have two different theories. The first, that you've been targeted for political reasons. The second, it's purely personal."

"Personal? How?"

"You've got an obsessed fan."

Chantal slowly sat down on one of the plain sofas covered in rich blue fabric and struggled to take it all in. She'd been poisoned. *Poisoned.* That meant someone had been close enough to get to her food, her drink...that same someone could go to the kitchen or the dining room without arousing suspicion.

"It's crazy," she finally concluded, her head reeling, fatigue growing. So much had happened in the past forty-eight hours. And now this news.

"What about Lilly?" she asked quietly, fear welling for her daughter. "Is there any suggestion that she, too, might be targeted?"

"No. Nothing. Her grandparents have her well protected." Demetrius crossed the floor, stood before her, looking down at her bent head. "It's you we're worried about. And we haven't ruled out that the threat might coming from the Thibaudets—"

"No."

"We can't rule it out, Princess. Both attempts on your life happened either at the châteaux, or nearby."

"No." Chantal stood, faced Demetrius, squaring off with him. "I haven't had a warm relationship with Armand's parents, but I know them, and I can't believe they'd ever be part of something so...reprehensible. They might be callous, but they're not malicious."

He said nothing. He simply stared at her, silently contradicting her and she flushed.

He'd be a ruthless adversary.

He'd never accept defeat.

"Queen Thibaudet practically grew up with my grandmother. They were childhood friends. The Thibaudets are essentially good people." Her voice came out husky, pathetically vulnerable.

"Good people that want custody of Lilly," he retorted flatly, without apology. "And they're tired of battling with you—"

"They don't battle with me. They've tied my hands completely!"

"Nonetheless, you worry them. You're a...thorn...in their side." His eyes narrowed, his wide jaw bristled by two day's growth of beard. "Haven't they told you as much?"

She closed her eyes. They had. But how did he know? She opened her eyes, looked briefly up, into his eyes, and then down at his chest. Far easier to keep her gaze there on the black shirt than his dark eyes which hinted at anger, and more. "How could you possibly have heard?"

"Every palace has ears."

A knock sounded on the door and a young maid appeared in the doorway. She bobbed her head and spoke to Demetrius in

Greek. Demetrius answered her and then turned to Chantal. "The doctor's here," he said. "He's waiting upstairs."

Demetrius stood at the far end of the bedroom, his back turned to give Chantal some privacy, while the doctor from Athens conducted a polite, professional examination. She'd been upset that Demetrius had insisted on remaining during the exam but she had to admit that he'd been as detached as humanly possible. The only time he'd glanced toward the bed was when the doctor had asked Chantal to sit up and she'd cried out at the stab of pain.

Chantal's cry had hardened Demetrius's jaw and he spoke quietly, harshly to the doctor, and the doctor immediately apologized to Chantal for causing her pain.

One of her eyebrows arched ever so slightly as she shot Demetrius an assessing glance. He was definitely in charge. Definitely the boss.

A few minutes later the doctor concluded the exam. He'd brought some painkillers with him and suggested the pills for pain relief, especially at night if the princess had difficulty sleeping. "Otherwise, I recommend rest," he said, closing his bag and drawing his suit jacket back on. "Her Highness needs to let the bruised muscles mend. Nothing too physical."

Demetrius walked the doctor out and then returned a few minutes later with the young Greek housemaid.

"This is Yolie," Demetrius said by way of introduction, "and she'll be assisting you while you're here."

Chantal felt as if her life had been completely taken over. First the doctor. Now the young Greek maid. "I don't need help."

"You can't sit up without whimpering like a baby, Princess—"

"Why do you call me that?" she interrupted, finding him overbearing. Arrogant. Controlling. Just the way he said princess put her teeth on edge. He never used Your Highness, or Your Royal Highness, the proper title of respect, much less addressed her with deference.

"What would you prefer? Your first name?"

Her bedroom seemed to have shrunk since he'd returned. She could almost see the white plaster walls move, the ceiling dropped. He dominated his space so completely. She refused to let him dominate her. "Your Highness, will do."

His upper lip curled. "Trying to put me in my place, Princess?"

She flushed, mortified that he'd not just recognized her intention, but called her on it, and she held her breath, battling her rage. She didn't want to be here. She wanted Lilly. She wanted peace. And if she couldn't have that, then she'd at least like to be alone. "I'd like some privacy, please. You may go."

"May I?"

"Yes. And you may take your housemaid with you. I'd prefer to be on my own."

"That's nice. Unfortunately I'm not leaving you alone, not when you're still so bruised. You'll need help drawing the bath and dressing. So drop the pride, and admit you need help—"

"I don't."

"You do. It's your choice. Yolie or me."

She drew in a swift breath. "You?"

His dark head inclined. "I'm more than happy to bathe and dress you."

His mocking tone made her see red. "As if I'd give you that opportunity!"

A warning light flared in his dark eyes. "You did yesterday."

"That's low."

Lines etched on either side of his firm mouth. "But true." He turned, walked to the door. But at the door he hesitated. "Just so you know, Yolie doesn't speak anything but Greek. If there's any confusion, feel free to send for me."

Right. He knew she'd never call for him. "Thank you."

He ignored her sarcasm. "Tonight I'll have dinner sent to your room so you can get some rest. But in the morning feel free to explore the house, and take advantage of the pool and gardens. The island is completely secure. You're welcome to relax or explore."

"I'll need some toiletries. Clothes."

"You'll find that the walk-in closet is lined with everything you could possibly wish for. Shorts, skirts, gowns, tracksuits, swimsuits from all the big designers."

"In my size?"

"Everything's your size. You're the fashion world's darling, and when the big designers heard you needed something to wear, the clothes poured in."

"In a day?"

He laughed. Grimly. "Don't underestimate yourself, Chantal. The clothes arrived within an hour. You're everybody's favorite princess."

CHAPTER SIX

FOR nearly a week after arriving on the island, Demetrius gave her the space she craved, as well as endless hours of time alone.

They didn't take meals together. They didn't sit down together for drinks or conversation. If they met, it was only in passing, and even then Chantal felt tense, awkward.

She wasn't just uncomfortable about what had happened between them. She was ashamed. The only comfort she found was the knowledge that what happened wasn't going to happen again. And the distance between then and now had helped her understand that the explosive chemistry between them had been a result of fear, fatigue, adrenaline. It wasn't normal, or natural, and the same situation wouldn't arise here on the Rock.

But still, she regretted her loss of control. She'd let someone in too close. She'd let Demetrius see—know—far too much of her life and it was dangerous. Dropping her boundaries for even a moment was dangerous.

A week after arriving on the Rock, Chantal left her bedroom and was heading downstairs when Demetrius appeared in the hall, dressed in faded black sweatpants and an old black T-shirt.

"I'd heard you were going for a walk," he said, standing at the bottom stair, waiting for her.

She froze half way down the staircase. They hadn't spoken in a couple of days and his sudden appearance—his very male appearance—unsettled her. He looked far too physical in the faded cotton sweats and T-shirt, the soft fabric clinging to the rugged planes of his chest, his biceps bare, his sweatpants sitting low on his hips, the sturdy cotton outlining the lean line of his thighs.

She knew what he looked like without the clothes, knew the golden skin underneath, knew the curve and knot of muscle. He'd feel warm. He'd feel hard. He'd feel too good.

It'd been a week since their night on Sao Tome and yet suddenly it felt like yesterday. "Yes," she answered, her breath strangled, and she smoothed her short green skirt flat against her thighs, wishing now it was a longer length. It'd looked crisp and fresh this morning in her closet but somehow Demetrius always made her feel exposed.

The nervous kneading of her hands drew his attention and he glanced at her thighs, noting the shortness of her dark green skirt and the length of bare, tan leg revealed.

"So you're feeling better?"

"Yes."

"Ribs not as sore?"

"Haven't had pain in a day or so."

He nodded, pleased. "Good. We'll get started then. You might want to change."

Her eyes narrowed and she eyed him warily. "Change for what?"

"Self-defense classes. It's essential. You have to know how to protect yourself." Demetrius gestured at her slim olive skirt. "So if you're going to change—"

"I'm not," she answered firmly, defiantly. She wasn't going to slip back into a submissive role. He was not in charge. He was not in control. "I'm quite comfortable as I am. Besides, this shouldn't take long."

He shrugged. "Fine. You're the princess."

He led her downstairs, to the bottom floor of the villa. She'd only been to the lower level once, and that was on her second day here. It was Demetrius's floor. She knew his office suite was downstairs, along with a spare bedroom, but she hadn't known about the gym.

The work out room was huge and surprisingly airy. The room accommodated all forms of exercise, from a wall of racked weights and benches to a state of the art treadmill and high tech exercise bike. In one corner a red punching bag hung from the ceiling, while bright blue mats covered nearly half the large hardwood floor.

"Come," he said, kicking off his running shoes at the door. "Join me on the mat."

Chantal removed her leather sandals and cautiously walked to where Demetrius waited for her on the bright blue rubber mat facing the mirror.

"First thing," he said, moving to stand behind her. "Is that you must be aware of your surroundings at all times. You must be conscious of where you are, and what's happening around you."

She nodded, skin tingling, acutely aware of him behind her, sensitive to everything about him. His size. His strength. The hard angle of his jaw.

"You have security detail. Bodyguards. Police escorts," he continued, stepping closer so that his breath brushed across the back of her neck, below her high ponytail. His breath was so warm on her skin and she balled her hands, willing herself not to shiver.

But when his arms encircled her, his hands resting on her hips she jerked violently.

"It's not enough to rely on others to protect you," he continued, his voice in her ear, his hands holding her hips securely. He'd always known how to hold her. Firmly. Calmly. With all the confidence in the world.

"Someone could get distracted," he was saying, even as her pulse raced, her head spinning with sensation.

He was relentless, she thought, his voice assaulting her, his body so warm behind hers.

"There could be another threat requiring immediate attention, your security might need to clear an obstacle, tackle an intruder, jump to protect Lilly. And in those moments you could be left completely exposed." His breath was caressing her neck, her skin, her body growing hotter by the second, her body betraying her yet again.

She burned at the feel of his hands, shuddered when his body came into contact with hers. She caught a glimpse of them in the mirror, Demetrius so large, towering over her, his big arms around her, his legs planted wide.

He was gorgeous and terrifying.

She could see his dark head tip as he spoke to her, saw the intensity in his expression, as well as the urgency.

Her mouth dried. She stared at them, the reflection of the two of them. She looked so small next to him, and it looked natural, too, as if they'd been carved from the same piece of stone, he on the outside, her on the inside, nestled against his chest.

"You need to know what you're going to do before it happens," he said, sliding his hands up her rib cage, wrapping his arms around her chest. "You need to know how you'll handle an attack, know the best way to break a hold. Like this," he said, his arms locked around her chest, his hands practically molding her breasts.

She tingled at the warmth of his hands against her breasts. It was like she had a million nerve endings, and they were all screaming, especially when he shifted and his hips brushed hers, his thighs nudging the back of hers.

"Feel this?" he asked.

She met his eyes in the mirror, mutely nodded. How could she not feel it? She was burning up. Her bare legs no match for the heat emanating from him.

"By the time someone has you trapped like this, it's over."

It was already over, she thought dizzily, heart racing, body trembling from head to toe. She might get off the island, return to royal life, but she'd never get over him.

He tightened his arms a fraction. "I've got your arms pinned to your side. My stance is too wide for you to kick backward, or connect with a knee."

For a moment they stood there, locked together, and again she met his gaze in the mirror and saw something so fierce, so intense in his expression that she wondered how she could have possibly thought that she could manage to control this...that she'd be able to indulge in a physical relationship with Demetrius and not be destroyed.

He wasn't going to let her go, she realized, panic rising. Not now. Not ever. He must have felt her panic because his arms abruptly fell away, and she was free.

Free, but not free. Safe, but not safe. She'd jumped from the fire into the frying pan. Chantal drew a quick breath, glanced at Demetrius.

His dark eyes rested on her. "I'm going to grab for you again," he said calmly. "When I make a grab for you this time, put your arms up, like this.'' He pulled his arms close to his chest, elbows in. ''Then as I bring my arms around, use your arms to break free. Push up and out.''

She did as he said, but she couldn't break free at all.

''Try it again.''

''I can't.''

''You can. Be aggressive, Chantal. You have to power up, shoot your arms out, think explosive.''

Explosive. That's exactly what she was thinking, but not the way he meant. Each time he touched her she shivered. Every time he spoke, his voice burrowed deep inside her, a honeyed heat that she found impossible to resist. She knew how it was in his arms, in his bed. She knew how his body moved against her...in her...she knew too well what he felt like, and how desperately she wanted to feel that passion and pleasure again and again.

I'm lost, she thought, dizzily. *I've never been in so much trouble in all my life.*

They practiced the move until he was satisfied—barely—and then it was another position, him wrapping his arms around her, lifting her bodily off the ground. ''Kick out, aim for my knee-cap,'' he said.

His chest was so hard against her back, his arms like steel bands.

''I don't want to hurt you,'' she panted.

''I'll take that chance.''

She felt like she was flailing in his arms, uncoordinated, gawky, weak. Her legs swung, trying to connect with him but unable to find a knee. ''This is ridiculous,'' she said, flushing, her breath coming hard. She didn't want to be fighting him. She didn't want to be in this horrid tug of war in the first place; and it was a war. This was passion versus reason.

She knew her desire for him was illogical. It was pure animal instinct, carnal and physical, and so unlike her real self she knew it'd never last.

''You're not trying,'' he charged.

''I am!''

He put her down, swung her around to face him, his hands resting on her shoulders. "This isn't a game, Princess."

She reached up, knocked his hands off her shoulders. "Don't you think I know that?" She shot back, humiliated. She couldn't understand what was happening inside of her, couldn't understand this crazy love-hate swamping her. "I'm trying. But this isn't natural for me. This isn't like anything I've ever done before."

"Yet another disservice at the hands of your family." His tone was harsh, cutting. "They did nothing to prepare you for reality, did they?"

"You know nothing about my life."

His eyes sparked. "I know all about powerful families, families where duty comes first; families where loyalty and obligation is everything."

"My grandparents did everything they could, and I'm very grateful to them—"

"For selling you off to their wealthy neighbor?"

"It was what was best—"

"For your family. For your country," he interrupted yet again, his voice grating across her nerves, his jaw tight. "Tell me, was saving everyone else worth it?"

"Yes." Her chin lifted. Her eyes met his, clashed, challenging him to contradict her again. "Yes. And I'd do it all over again if asked."

"You're kidding yourself."

And if she was? It was no business of his. He was her bodyguard, dammit. Not her partner. And most certainly not her husband. "Why do you even care?"

"Why don't you care more?"

She shook her head, momentarily speechless. "You have more opinions than any man I've ever met."

He was breathing hard now. "I might have a lot of opinions, but I back up my talk with action."

Her hands balled at her sides. "Unfortunately for you, Demetrius, there doesn't seem to be anyone you can beat up right now."

"Maybe it's you that needs a good swat on your pert little behind."

"Oh!" She seethed with indignation. "I think I need some different company." Marching to the door, she jammed her right foot into one sandal and then the left. "I'm going for a walk," she said in a strangled voice. "And don't follow me. If this is really your island, your *Rock,* then I ought to be perfectly safe getting some fresh air!"

Chantal swiftly climbed the stairs back to the main level, exited the villa through the front door, and crossed the driveway, walking down the long winding driveway. Her eyes were filling with wretched tears and she silently cursed herself, cursed Demetrius, cursed the fact that she—who never used to cry—had become one massive tear duct.

She hated him.

Absolutely positively hated him.

No one else had ever gotten under her skin this way. No one else had ever made her feel so helpless...so confused...so completely off balance. It only took a couple words from him, one long searing glance, and she fell apart, dissolving into a tearful, jagged mass of emotion.

The fact that he had such power over her scared her. Made her furious. Made her want to scream.

Chantal stumbled on a rock and righting herself, laughed at her stupidity. Of course Demetrius was right. Of course it horrified her that she'd married only to lose herself, married only to be destroyed. But it wasn't supposed to have happened that way. It was supposed to be a real marriage. A good marriage. A good life.

She shook her head, hating these thoughts, unable to remember the past, unable to look too far into the future. She never used to dwell on her life this way. She never thought about herself at all. But something had happened the night the plane veered off course, shuddering, shimmying. It was as if the plane on breaking apart had broken something loose inside of her.

The plane was wrecked.

Her world was shattered.

And who was going to fix her? The plane could be replaced,

but what about her? What about this *wanting?* How in God's name would she ever stop feeling now that she'd started?

Demetrius swore beneath his breath, standing on the terrace on the main level watching his princess strut down the driveway, her slender legs bare to mid thigh, her skin the color of sun kissed wheat, her long dark hair swept up in a ponytail high at the back of her head.

He'd never met a more sassy thing. He swore bitterly again. She was making him crazy. She was making him burn.

She was nothing like Katina, either. Katina was blonde, dark olive skin, shy. *Sweet.*

Chantal might long to be reserved, and she played the ice queen well, but she wasn't sweet.

No, she wasn't sweet. She was hot, she was intense, she was smart.

And he wanted her like he'd never wanted anyone. He'd tried to stay away from her. He'd tried to keep his distance, but his self-control was wearing thin.

Very, very thin.

Chantal left the road where it merged onto a smaller path, the grass trampled flat, and followed the dirt path as it began to slope downhill.

She'd had it with men. She didn't want them. Didn't need them. Didn't want anything but to be free. And alone.

She tramped on, arms swinging, temper surging, the warm sun overhead making her thirsty.

If she'd been a real woman, she told herself, she would have told Armand to get lost. If she'd been a real woman, she would have set him straight. She would have left him the first time he raised a hand against her. Instead she tried to reason with him, and then before she knew it, she was pregnant, and the baby changed everything.

Because the baby trapped her in La Croix. Even if she left La Croix, the baby would be Armand's heir.

She should have left him the first time he lost his temper like that, should have packed her bags and headed home and never looked back.

Why did she wait? Why did she hesitate? Love. She'd once loved him enough to imagine a happy life with him. And then when the love was dashed by misery, she still found hope, and hope made her believe that something good could come of her pain. That something good might still happen for her one day. Chantal shook her head slowly, overwhelmed by the endless memories, the mountain of regrets.

The path continued to drop, descend, and rounding the side of the hill Chantal glimpsed the sea again, and then a cluster of houses and whitewashed buildings along a narrow road.

Small red and blue boats were tethered to a low stone wall. Goats grazed in a pasture behind several of the houses. A little tavern with blue painted tables and chairs overlooked the water, hugging rocky land between the road and sea. It was a real Greek village, a charming little town with a shop and tavern and dark-haired children playing football in the street.

She'd been here a week and hadn't even known it existed. Pausing at the edge of the village, Chantal watched the boys. Life in Melio was like this. Little boys teasing girls in the street, little girls sticking out their tongues, little boys growing up into teenagers with crushes on the teenage girls.

One of the boys spotted Chantal and picked up the black and white ball, holding it against his hip. The other boys turned and stared at her.

She felt a funny flutter in the middle of her chest. She was obviously a stranger here, and for a moment she was tempted to turn back around and climb up the hill again, but on the top of the hill was Demetrius and his big whitewashed house that perched above the sea like a predatory bird about to take flight.

No. She wasn't going to go back to the house. She'd walked all the way here. She was going to go on into the village and get some air, and some much needed space.

Space away from Demetrius Mantheakis. Because somehow he'd taken over her life, taken over her thoughts, her heart, her body, too.

She felt the eyes on her as she crossed the dusty road, stepping onto a cobbled sidewalk that must have been part of the island for hundreds of years.

Ducking beneath a canvas awning, she entered the taverna's patio and took a seat at one of the empty tables close to the ocean.

There were four or five older men seated at a table close to the bar. They all stopped talking to look at her, a long measured glance that took in her short linen skirt the color of olives, her fitted white T-shirt, her hair caught up in a high ponytail with wisps now sliding down her neck.

She mustered a smile as she pulled a chair out, but they didn't smile back. Their weathered faces remained perfectly blank. *Fine. Be that way.* Ignoring them she sat down. Leaned on the table. Looked around. Waited. And waited. And waited some more.

Minutes passed, a good five, ten minutes, and yet no one approached her. No one appeared from the kitchen. The young man behind the long bar never made eye contact.

Chantal felt her temper rise. It was hot. Flushed and sticky from the walk, she really craved a cold drink—and some service please. Standing, she crossed the floor, walked to the bar. "I'd like to see a menu, please."

The bartender had been washing out coffee cups and reluctantly he turned the water off. "A menu?"

She hid her impatience. She spoke French, Spanish, English, German and Italian. Surely he understood the word menu. "I'd like to order something to eat."

The young Greek bartender had thick wavy black hair that fell across his forehead, long dark lashes, and he stared at her as if she were an alien being, then he looked at the group of older men sitting at the table in the shade. One of the older men said something to the bartender and the bartender shrugged.

Suddenly another voice spoke sharply in Greek and everyone shifted into action. *Demetrius.*

The bartender flushed, the old men at the table, shifted their feet, murmured apologetic words in Greek, and Demetrius moved toward her. "I'm sorry. You shouldn't have been treated like that."

He'd drawn her chair out for her and reluctantly she sat back down. If it'd been tense in the taverna before, it was doubly nerve-racking now. "They don't like me?"

He shrugged. "It was a misunderstanding. That's all." But that wasn't all, she thought. The energy in the tavern, at their table, had changed, become charged, electric.

"He wasn't going to serve me," she added, trying to understand the undercurrents.

"No." Demetrius leaned on the table, looked at her, his gaze hard, heated. "They know you're off-limits."

"Off-limits?"

He leaned even closer so they were just inches apart, his dark eyes burning into her, telling her with his eyes what he hadn't yet said with his lips. "They know, *pedhaki mou,* you're mine."

Her heart hammered wildly. He was so close. She could see each dense black eyelash, the tiny bits of copper reflecting in his dark brown eyes. "But I'm not yours." Her voice came out faint.

He simply stared at her, his upper lip barely curving. It was the coolest, most sardonic smile she'd seen in her life; a smile so cool, so sardonic she was forced to look away, hands clasped beneath her chin to keep her wildly beating heart in control.

"You're here," he said softly. "Actions, not words."

Still looking away, Chantal swallowed hard, stared at the line of sand and sea. If she were completely honest she'd admit that the danger waiting for her in La Croix seemed far more manageable than the danger sitting across the table.

Cold drinks arrived. Then a basket of breads and crackers appeared, soon followed by goat cheese, olives, and marinated vegetables.

Life here was like a medieval village. She reached for a hunk of the crusty bread, tore off a piece and dipped it in the fragrant olive oil.

They ate an early lunch, and after they were finished Demetrius leaned back, and watched Chantal. She'd relaxed, he thought, studying her. She'd dropped her guard long enough to enjoy the village, and he could see her take in everything, from the two fishermen down at the water to the group of men at the table next to them.

One of the men nearby laughed, a deep hearty laugh and Chantal looked at Demetrius.

"Zeno," he said. "Our resident Papa."

Chantal smiled at his explanation, a tiny dimple flashing at the corner of her mouth and his gut tightened.

He wasn't going to let this get out of control again. Not even when she looked at him like that, with a shy glance so full of need and want from beneath her thick dark lashes, her eyes half-smiling up at him, her eyes a warm French blue. She was beautiful—elegant, refined, sophisticated. And yet when he looked into her eyes he saw a world of sadness she prayed no one would see, and most people wouldn't see it, most men wouldn't know what it was, but he recognized the starkness of the pain that made her eyes an even more startling blue.

She'd had her heart crushed, and like the young woman she'd been, she hadn't even seen it coming. Women, he'd learned, were nothing like men. Women looked forward to love and marriage because it was going to be cozy...warm...happy. They were going to be beautiful brides and beloved young wives and then the first of the cherished babies would come along...

Demetrius turned his head away, looked out at the dark blue water and the sailboat sailing across the sparkling waves.

Katina had been like that, too. She'd been so happy to be with him, so happy to be married to him. They didn't have long together, just two and a half years. She was pregnant when she died. Seven and a half months.

His mouth filled with bitterness, the acid of old. There had never been an hour where he could forget. He'd been raised to be a man, and men wanted to protect those more vulnerable. They were driven to protect their women, their children...

Chantal's hand touched his arm. "Demetrius."

The red glaze that filmed his eyes faded away. He turned to look at Chantal. She barely came to his shoulder and her thick glossy brown hair gathered in that high ponytail made her look young, far younger than her thirty years.

She was still so innocent, he thought, still so naive. Without thinking he reached out, combed a stray tendril of hair from her dusty rose cheek.

She blushed, her gaze dropping. He couldn't imagine how anyone could raise a hand against her. Couldn't imagine how Armand could do anything but protect her.

Her lashes lifted and she looked back up at him, an uncertain smile curving her lips.

"Have you ever been married?"

"Once." His features looked closed, unreadable.

"Why didn't you ever marry again?"

"Not interested."

"Was your marriage that bad?"

"No. It was that good."

"Oh." She ducked her head again, and she looked so wistful, so much like a kid outside a candy store.

"Would you marry again?" he asked, watching her eyes widen, the sapphire blue so much like the sea.

Her expression immediately shuttered, the veil dropping back over her eyes, hiding thought, emotion, turning her back into the remote ice princess. "No."

"Why not?" he persisted.

Color darkened her cheeks but she looked agonized. "The whole princess thing scares people."

That wasn't it at all, he thought, feeling something inside him wrench. She was lying to him, lying to herself, deliberately twisting the truth.

Her marriage had been horrible. Marriage had scarred her. Scared her.

Aware of a new tension within him, Demetrius leaned forward, rested his weight on the table, moving closer to Chantal, close enough to see all the skin her small T-shirt hadn't covered, the shadow between her breasts and the small golden brown freckle on her collarbone.

He'd never tell her that her vulnerability moved him. That her isolation profoundly touched him.

A princess with her wealth, and her beauty, could have been cold, and yet Chantal was the opposite.

Her softness was everywhere—in her eyes, her lips, in the yearning in her expression. She reminded him of a girl who jumped from childhood to adulthood without a parachute, or the necessary years between.

''I'm not scared,'' he said quietly, feeling her body hum, watching her face, her emotions barely veiled. ''You're a woman, not a machine.''

Chantal's mask suddenly dropped and for a split-second she looked at him with outright longing. The loneliness in her eyes cut him. She'd been abandoned too many years ago. Adrift too long.

His body burned. His fingers itched. He wanted to take her face between his hands and kiss her. Kiss her until she melted into him, until those high walls around her fell, kiss her until she warmed, her body and heart as hot as his.

''We've company, boss.'' The young bartender's voice rang out, breaking the tense silence.

Looking up, Demetrius saw the bartender had binoculars fixed on a point out at sea. ''What do you see?'' Demetrius demanded, attention abruptly shifted.

''A boat. And it's heading our way.''

CHAPTER SEVEN

CHANTAL heard the flurry of Greek, the immediate rise in tension as well as the strange, taut silence that suddenly enveloped them.

Everyone had gone quiet, even the older men. Every head turned to face the sea, all eyes squinting against the sun and the dazzling reflection on the unbelievably turquoise water.

Awareness filled the taverna and Chantal glanced from one man to the next. Something was wrong.

She heard Demetrius speak, Greek words spoken so low and quickly, that she didn't have a hope of understanding, but his tone was unmistakable. He didn't like what he saw.

The pair of young fishermen down at the water also stopped stowing their nets and they, too, faced the water.

What was out there?

Chantal was tempted to rise, but her training was too deeply ingrained. Don't ask too many questions. Don't pry. Don't get involved in business that isn't your own.

But the relaxed atmosphere at the tavern had disappeared. Every man faced the water, waiting.

It was a boat. A small, private sailboat, and it was heading straight to the tiny harbor.

As all eyes stared intently at the cove, a man on board the sailboat dropped anchor and then jumped over the yacht's edge, into the relatively shallow water. He waded toward the low stone retaining wall and the men at the tavern closed ranks around the princess.

Chantal felt the strain, the stress palpable. She could hardly see the beach anymore, but one of the older men from the tavern rose. He was big, burly, the man Demetrius had called Zeno. Zeno headed toward the water, intercepting the young sailor before he could reach the tavern.

"This is a private island." Zeno's deep voice carried. "You're trespassing."

Chantal couldn't hear what the young man was saying, but he was talking, gesturing to his boat, his hands now making shapes in the air, and Zeno didn't look as if he gave a damn. His dark head shook, his arms folded across his chest. "We don't fix boats. Sorry."

The sailor answered and then laughed.

Zeno wasn't laughing.

The sailor tried to brush past Zeno whose arm shot out, grabbed the man by the shoulder and suddenly the sailor was lying flat on his back.

Chantal winced. She saw Demetrius's right hand flex but he didn't move. He wasn't going to leave her side.

"We don't fix boats," Zeno repeated, slowly, loudly, his foot on the sailor's chest. "You need to leave now. Understand?" The man finally understood, whether he wanted to or not. And with Zeno's not so friendly assistance, returned to his boat without further delay.

"That was quite a display of power," she said, completely unnerved. The Rock was like no place she'd ever been before.

Demetrius shrugged. "Everyone works hard here to keep the island safe." With the sailboat disappearing on the horizon, he extended a hand to her. "Come. Let's walk a bit."

But Chantal was still shaken. Demetrius's men had collectively banded together, formed a human shield. She didn't know how Demetrius and his islanders had formed such an intense relationship, but he was right. These were his people. They would protect him, and the island, at all costs.

Demetrius stood next to the table, his brow furrowed as he gazed down at her. "You're not afraid, are you?"

Yes, she wanted to answer him, yes, I am afraid. I've been afraid for years. But whom could she talk to? Whom could she confide in?

"There's nothing to worry about," he continued, his tone softening somewhat. "My people will not let any harm come to you."

She suddenly wished she'd known someone like Demetrius years ago, back when she was still a wife, back when she cringed with fear every time Armand lifted his voice—or his hand. She would have liked to have someone like Demetrius on her side. She would have welcomed his strength. His courage. His counsel.

But there hadn't been anyone like Demetrius then, and she couldn't have him now. She was trapped, and she knew it.

"You're right," she said, forcing a smile to her lips, her face feeling stiff, numb. She couldn't explain the wild swing of emotion, couldn't explain how the physical awareness had turned to something else, how hunger had suddenly given way to a vast emotional need. "Everything's fine."

Rising, Chantal felt self conscious all over again. She couldn't bear being here with him like this. She hated that his company— and even his attempt to comfort her—only reinforced her loneliness. Her wretched inner emptiness. She hated these emotions, hated feeling broken. Once she'd been the strong one in the family. The leader. The big sister. The role model.

She wanted to laugh at the irony. In the end, she was the worst sort of role model. She was a disaster. Spineless. Shattered.

They left the taverna and stepped outside into the bright sunshine. The hard glaze of light momentarily blinded Chantal and she lifted a hand to shield her eyes.

"Need sunglasses?" Demetrius asked.

"No." She actually welcomed the intense light. The sun burned her eyes, imprinting little gold halos against her eyelids, but the brightness, and the heat, chased away some of the clouds within her. She couldn't very well go through life feeling sorry for herself. Yes, her marriage had been painful, but she had a beautiful daughter, a daughter she loved more than life itself.

They walked for a few minutes in silence, and until today Chantal would have never known that the island had another face to it. There was the side she knew well, the black volcanic rock, the arid steep pitch of land emerging from the sea, and then there was this, the softer face, the one that supported a small village with a tiny fleet of fishing boats and the traditional taverna on the beach.

"Tell me more about Lilly," Demetrius said, as they crossed the sand, walked along the low stone wall, the breeze coming in off the water smelling sharp and salty. "What does your daughter like to do?"

"Play games," she answered, putting out her hands to balance her as she climbed up on top of the old wall. They were passing the fishermen and the two young men nodded at Demetrius but otherwise continued working.

"She must have some beautiful dolls."

"She has a couple dolls, but I try to keep the expensive playthings to a minimum."

"Her grandparents spoil her."

She shrugged uneasily, and glanced back over her shoulder at the quaint village. "I don't want her to get used to grand gestures."

"Toys are grand gestures?"

"They're deceptive. Just like fairy tales."

"And you don't read her those, either?"

"Maybe I shouldn't anymore."

He shot her a quizzical glance. "And what would you do instead?"

"Teach her karate. Some of those self-defense moves you were trying to teach me."

He laughed, thank goodness, his dark gaze smiling down at her. "Are you admitting that I might possibly be right about something?"

She bent down, picked up a broken seashell, rubbed the water softened edge against her hand. "You're right about a lot of things. I just don't want it to go to your head. Your ego's mammoth as it is."

"*My* ego?"

"*Massive.*"

He laughed again. It was so unlike him, so unlike the person he'd become. He watched Chantal jump off the wall into the packed sand and head for the water. He followed her, pursuing her to the water's edge.

She was gazing out across the water, and the breeze grabbed the hem of her short skirt, revealing even more of the back of her knees and her slim, bare thighs. His body responded, desire tightening within him, making him feel hard, impatient. He was tired of holding back. Resisting his attraction, resisting her, was wearing him down. But he wasn't the only one wearing down.

Chantal's tension was tangible. Palpable. He could feel her frustration. She wanted off the island. He was keeping her on. She wanted away from him. He wouldn't give her the chance.

But he was doing this for her, he reminded himself, he was doing what he had to do. "My marriage was arranged, too," he said abruptly, not at all sure why he was sharing some private information.

Chantal was intrigued. She faced him, blue eyes wide. "Really?"

"Greek families like mine do it all the time. Arranged marriages bring families closer together. Solidify wealth. Power. I hadn't wanted to marry Katina. She wasn't my first choice—even though she was very pretty—but in the end it worked. Better than anyone expected."

"So your family did a good job."

"With Katina, yes."

Chantal stared at him, incredibly curious. "What did your family do that you didn't like?"

"The list is too long to even start. My family—" He broke off, crossed his arms over his chest, muscles hardening in his arms, biceps curving, triceps thickening. The hair on his arms was dark, semicoarse and his skin was tanned, his wrist was wide and the black and gold watch just emphasized the width and strength of his bones. "My family is well known. Everyone here knows them. They know me. They know who I am, what I've done—"

"What *did* you do?"

Demetrius turned, his body inches from her. The warm wind lifted his thick black hair and she could smell the musky spice of his skin. She'd never met anyone who smelled like he did and the more she was around him the more she found herself wanting to breathe in the scent that was spicy and strong and somehow, oddly, sexual.

"I wasn't always in the business I am now." His dark eyes were nearly as hard as his jaw. "I come from a very old Greek family with very old ties."

She nodded, indicating the sprawling Greek villa on the cliff behind them. "But you were raised with money?"

"This I earned." His lashes lowered, his expression shuttered. "But yes, there was money. Plenty of money. But we didn't wear our wealth like the nouueau riche. We were a very private family, and in our family, you stayed within the family, worked within the family."

She was trying to read between the lines, and there was a lot being written between the lines. He'd mentioned how private and closed his family was a couple of times. "What did you do for your family?"

The corner of his mouth lifted. "More than you'd want to know."

She met his gaze. "And your family was in which business?"

"All of them."

The hair on her nape rose, a prickling that laced through her middle. "But you don't work for your family anymore?"

"No." His lashes dropped, and as he stared past her shoulder, his jaw wide, a small muscle knotting, popping near his ear. "And what I do now is important. It helps people, doesn't hurt them."

His head turned, his gaze dropping, his dark eyes resting on her face. "I had disturbing news this morning, Chantal."

She went hot, then cold. "Lilly?"

"No."

His answer sent relief surging through her but the rush of adrenaline was almost too much. Her legs felt quivery and weak.

"Let's sit," he said, indicating the low stone wall and she didn't argue, her knees bending, her weight sinking onto the rough wall.

Demetrius sat down next to her. "There's no easy way to say this, Chantal, so let me say it quickly. You know there have been threats against you, including physical threats. Apparently another one was made, and this one resulted in a fatality."

Chantal sat motionless, her arms at her sides. *A fatality?* Demetrius's shocking words reverbrated around her head like a gong against a steel drum.

A fatality? To whom? How? Her heart hammered so hard she thought she'd throw up. With difficulty she forced herself to swallow the awful cold lump that filled her throat, blocking air, slowing thought. "What happened?"

"Someone tampered with your car—" he broke off, jaw flexed, and continued "—the bomb exploded when the ignition was turned. Your young driver, Tanguy, was killed."

Tanguy. Killed? He was just twenty. No more than a boy. "Car bomb?"

"Someone has too much access to you." Demetrius's voice sounded harsh. "Someone knows too much about you."

But she wasn't thinking about herself, or her safety. She was thinking about Tanguy. Remembering how he'd turned twenty only a month ago, remembering how he'd told her about the birthday party his girlfriend had thrown him, remembering how the night of his party he and his friends had stayed up until morning celebrating their friendship and life.

And now he was gone?

"Why was he in my car?" Chantal's eyes filmed with tears. She could barely breathe. "He doesn't drive my car. He drives me in one of the palace sedans."

Demetrius hesitated. His features were hard, his expression shuttered. "He was taking it round to be washed, detailed. He thought you'd be home soon and he wanted to surprise you."

And now he's dead.

Chantal covered her face, pressed the palms of her hands against her eyes.

She felt his hand on her shoulder, his fingers gripping her shoulder blade. "You're going to be safe," he said quietly. "You will be safe here, and we won't return you to La Croix until we know for certain you'll be safe there."

"I'm not worried about me," she answered, dropping her hands. "It's Tanguy. He died because of me."

"You can't think like that. You have to concentrate on safety. Survival. Concentrate on getting through this so you can return to Lilly."

Lilly. Just her name was a touchstone, a reminder of what she needed, what she loved, and Chantal's heart burned. "I miss her."

"I know." He stood. "Let's go back to the villa. We have work to do."

For the next four days Demetrius spent hours training Chantal, teaching her moves, blocks, defensive steps, as well as offensive attacks.

On the fifth day he opened up a locked cabinet, revealing an extensive weapon collection. She immediately recoiled. "I don't like those."

"You're not supposed to," he answered flatly. But that didn't stop him from withdrawing the weapons, showing her how they worked, the damage they inflicted.

He also taught her how to minimize the assault from various weapons, and his relentless explanations, his intensive training, peeled off the protective outer layer and left her feeling deeply exposed.

She'd known nothing about survival, she thought wearily. She'd learned numerous foreign languages, studied art, music, history, fashion, culture. But she didn't know the first thing about protecting herself.

Or Lilly.

And she was missing Lilly, more and more. Chantal's inside churned constantly, her emotions pulled. It'd been over two weeks now since she'd last seen her daughter.

But it wasn't just missing Lilly that was wearing Chantal down. She felt the most ambivalent emotions around Demetrius. All the hours in training had kept them in almost constant contact.

For days now their bodies touched. Their skin brushed. Their thoughts came together.

Yet this was business. He was all business. Professional, cool, detached. And yet his detachment was worse than his passion. After being so intimate, feeling so physically close, she didn't know how to ignore the current of desire running through her. Didn't know if she could ever forget what he'd made her feel.

Or what his touch made her realize she'd sacrificed.

To be the good, dutiful wife, to be the obedient daughter-in-law, she'd denied herself everything she needed. And it was only now, lying flat on her back on the thick spongey mat in his gym, her body warm, damp with perspiration, she realized she'd been living in a sterile metal box for the past years, denied of sound, touch, sensation, love.

Love. She'd never thought she'd find it, never thought she'd dare to hope for more of anything, but somehow isolated here on Demetrius's Rock, she'd begun to dream again. And the dreams frightened her. The dreams teased her, reminding her of who she'd once been, of what she'd once imagined.

"Are you okay?" Demetrius asked, reaching down to extend a hand to her.

"Yes." She was still panting from the exertion of the exercise, and she let him help pull her to her feet.

"Let's call it a day. I've been working you hard. You've earned some time off."

"You're sure?" she answered lightly, trying to hide the crazy conflicting emotion inside of her. She loved being near him. She hated being near him. She wanted more. She couldn't have more.

"Positive. I'm a nice guy. Sometimes." He handed her a towel and her bottled water. "I'll see you at dinner."

"Fine."

But in her bedroom she didn't feel fine. She felt wild. Desperate. Emotional.

She wanted so much right now it terrified her. She wanted so much that her need made her feel primitive. Animal-like.

Where was Chantal Ducasse Thibaudet? Where was the cool, contained woman she'd once been?

In his study, Demetrius stood next to his desk, staring down at the letters he'd just read. The stack of letters was far larger than he'd expected. There were dozens of letters, all written to the princess, all intercepted by the Melio palace security.

The letters were by hand, and they were long, and rambling. The tone of each was downright creepy. Even accustomed to creeps and freaks, Demetrius felt a chill spread through his middle as he reviewed the letters.

Bits and pieces jumped out at him. *You belong to me, Chantal. We belong together. No one loves you like I do.*

He switched letters.

I can't live without you. I have to have you. I have to be with you. I know you feel the same.

Another letter.

Darling, cherie, why don't you answer? Why play these games? You must stop these games now. Come to me immediately. I don't want to be angry with you. My darling, Chantal, you are very wicked to hurt me like this. Don't make me punish you. I don't want to hurt you.

The letters had been sent over a period of three months. The first letters were postmarked roughly two weeks apart, but after awhile they became increasingly frequent until the sender was writing a letter daily.

It didn't help that the letters showed increasing disintegration—moving from hopeful fantasy, to projection of fantasy, to threats of intimidation and violence.

Demetrius reached for the last letter, received by the palace only a few days ago. *Don't think you can escape me, Chantal. Don't think you'll ever escape me. If I can't have you, no one will. Do you understand? If I can't have you, no one will.*

But the man was wrong, Demetrius thought, studying the last letter, the handwriting jagged, erratic, matching the writer's anger and obsession, before restacking the letters and binding them with a rubber band. No one was going to get close enough to Chantal to hurt her. They'd have to go through him first.

She'd bathed, rested, and now Chantal sorted through the clothes in her closet trying to find something appropriate for dinner.

It was her twelfth night on the island, her fifth dinner with Demetrius, her fifth quiet evening where her body would feel hot, cold, painfully alive. Her fifth night where she'd sit there wanting Demetrius to look at her, wanting him to talk to her. Wanting him to want her the way she wanted him.

The dinners together had become a kind of agony. She felt like a teenager again, overcome with hopeless longing. He had no idea, either.

Chantal wondered what he'd think if he knew she sat at the table each night fantasizing about him pulling her into a semidark hallway, pressing her up against the wall, and kissing her as if there was no tomorrow.

Her stomach tensed, her whole body tightening with need. She thought she'd die if she didn't kiss him again soon. She needed something to ease the pressure building inside of her.

Taking a long pale apricot dress from the closet, Chantal held it up to the light, studied the silky apricot folds. She could see herself in this, see Demetrius's hands against her skin, imagine him shaping her against him.

Her skin tingled. Her breasts felt so sensitive. It'd been so long since she felt raw and carnal like this, and the fierceness of her desire made her nerves scream. What was this emotion anyway? Was this love...lust...infatuation?

She put the dress back. Bit her lip. All she knew was that she wanted him. And she wanted him to want her. But she also wanted more than that.

Eyes prickling, stinging, she blinked to keep the tears from falling. She wanted love and sex and no tomorrow. Love and sex and one long endless night.

She wanted a night of no regrets. A night without mistakes. A night to end all nights...

But that's not going to happen, she angrily answered herself, hating how violent she felt on the inside. She was flooded with hormones, overwhelmed by needs that had never been met. She was acting so silly, acting girlish and young, and yet she was thirty. *Thirty*. How could she confuse physical attraction with emotional needs? How could she imagine that sex—even great sex—would be the answer to anything?

Impatient with herself, Chantal dragged a long blue and cream dress from the closet and carried it to her bed. After donning lace panties in the palest shade of blue, she slipped into the long designer gown. The dress was a mix of small silk patterns, the fabric shades of cream and French Provincial blue. The slender silhouette of the gown gave way at the knees to a slight flare, and the silk fabric had been beaded at the bodice, a stunning geometric pattern of blue beading, open at the neckline in a classic keyhole shape.

Nothing about the dress was expected, nothing traditional, and yet the lightness of the fabric, the exquisite beading, the gorgeous neckline made it a work of art.

Calmer, Chantal faced herself in the mirror, and looking at her reflection, her cheeks a dusty rose from the afternoons in the sun, she knew it wasn't just sex she wanted. She wanted sex, and love, and a chance to live a real life, a life where she'd be an ordinary woman with ordinary dreams.

She wanted a life where someone good and strong would love her. She wanted a life where a man would treasure her, adore her, protect her. She wanted a man who'd love her—heart, mind, body and soul.

You're no better than your little sister, Joelle, Chantal silently mocked, picking up her hairbrush, and brushing her long hair until it rippled and gleamed. Her hand pausing midair, she stared at herself, trying to see what it was about her that angered Armand so much, what it was in her face that made photographers shadow her, what it was that Lilly saw when she looked up at her.

Her long dark hair was now shot with streaks of burnished copper, and her skin glowed gold from the time in the sun, but her blue eyes were still quiet. Sad. Too sad. She hated the sadness. She was ready to move on with her life. Ready to go home. Ready to be with Lilly.

Lilly. Her heart squeezed, her breath catching in her throat. God, she missed her. When she thought about Lilly the pain was almost too much.

Indeed, all of it had become too much. Tonight Chantal's heart felt broken.

Downstairs Demetrius stood on the terrace, facing the sea, his back to the house. He'd dressed for dinner, black trousers, crisp white linen shirt, the sleeves casually rolled up on his forearms. He was on his cell phone, and she felt a pang. How lucky to be able to just call up whomever he wanted, when he wanted. He must have heard her footsteps because he turned. Nodded at her. But instead of hanging up, he held the phone to her.

"You've someone who can't go to bed until you wish her good night."

Chantal went hot, cold. She looked up into Demetrius's face, unable to believe what he was telling her.

He smiled reassuringly. "Your daughter's waiting."

CHAPTER EIGHT

JUST when she'd thought she couldn't take anymore, just when the emptiness threatened to overwhelm her, she'd been given this gift.

Her eyes met Demetrius. She struggled to speak, wanted to thank him, but the words wouldn't come.

"She's waiting," he reminded her gently.

Chantal nodded, and shaking, she took the phone from him. "Lilly?" she choked, tears streaming as Lilly's voice echoed across the phone line.

"Mommy!" Lilly cried. "Mommy, Mommy!"

It was almost too much. Chantal ground her teeth together. Lilly was her heart. "How are you, baby?"

"Good. I miss you."

"I miss you so much, too."

For the next ten minutes they chatted about everything. It seemed that Auntie Joelle had gone to La Croix to spend a long weekend with Lilly, and Chantal offered up a silent prayer of thanks to her sister. And in the next breath, Lilly chattered on about all the things she was doing—music lessons, dance lessons, school lessons, language lessons. Lilly had always been kept very busy at the Thibaudets' insistence.

"But when are you coming home?" Lilly demanded at last. "I want you here. I want you home."

"And I want to be home, too," Chantal answered, her heart full to bursting. She drew a breath, steadied her voice. "It won't be long until I'm back."

"Promise?"

"Yes." The tears filled her eyes yet again, but she held them back. "Be good, sweetheart. Listen to your grandparents."

"I do."

"I know. I just—" she broke off, squeezed her eyes closed,

pressed a hand to her mouth. She couldn't do this, couldn't say goodbye.

A steady hand touched her back, and she looked up, saw Demetrius, saw encouragement in his warm dark gaze.

She drew a deep breath, calmed herself. "I love you," she said at last, her voice stronger. "And I can't wait to see all the things you've learned and done while I've been gone. Will you try to remember everything and tell me as soon as I'm home?"

"I'll draw you a picture."

Her heart tugged. "Will you?".

"I'll draw lots. I'll make you a picture book so you can see everything."

"I'd love that. I really would."

There was a moment of silence on the line and then Lilly spoke, her own voice suddenly deeper, more serious. "I love you, Mommy."

It was as if Lilly had grown up over night. Chantal bit her lip, pictured Lilly's face, could see the furrow between her light brown eyebrows. "I love you, baby. Sleep tight."

"You, too, Mommy. Bye bye."

Bye bye. Silently Chantal handed the phone back to Demetrius. She couldn't look at him. She had to look away, out toward the water where another stunning sunset played out across the dark blue waves.

"Thank you." Her voice was hoarse, the tears still there, buried in her heart. "That was the nicest gift ever."

He said nothing for a moment, pocketing the phone. His features looked drawn. "It was your sister," he said roughly. "She traveled to La Croix knowing we needed her help to get the call placed."

"She didn't have to do that."

"Of course not. But your sisters adore you. Both of them. I've been speaking with them both all week—"

"You have?"

"And you're their hero," he continued, as if she'd never interrupted. "They'd do anything for you."

"But I'm the big sister," she said, trying to move forward, not wanting to linger on a topic like this when her emotions were already dangerously high. Talking to Lilly had undone her, made her feel so many things.

"Even big sisters need help." He continued to regard her with that intense, piercing gaze. "And your sisters hate that your late husband hurt you."

She stiffened, surprised, flustered. "He's gone. It doesn't matter anymore."

There was a moment of silence. "It doesn't matter that your husband was physically abusive?"

She looked up, around, feeling wildly disorganized. It made her queasy, talking about this, and they still had dinner ahead. "He wasn't a bad person, he just had a problem with his temper, and he always apologized later. He didn't like to lose his temper."

Demetrius let her babble on, his face impassive and yet he hated what she was saying. She didn't even know what she was saying. She wasn't the cause of her husband's anger, just the scapegoat. Yet Armand had successfully destroyed her self-confidence so she couldn't stand up for herself. "You aren't to blame for your husband's weaknesses. Your husband had the problem. Not you."

"But I am still to blame," she said softly. "I wanted us to be a family. I kept thinking if I could figure out what I was doing wrong, we'd be a real family, and that idea of family meant everything to me."

"Why?"

"I don't know. Maybe because I had family taken away from me too young." So of course it crushed her when she realized her new family despised her. It had never crossed her mind the Thibaudets would hate her. Why should they? They'd chosen her.

Demetrius saw her lips twist, a small self-mocking smile that burrowed deep inside of him.

"Family is important," he agreed, feeling the rage claw at him. He, too, would have done anything to protect his family. He'd been prepared to trade his life for Katina's. It'd been the most natural—instinctive—thing to do. "But you sacrificed yourself—"

"I had to."

"You didn't. And if you really believe that, then your family sold you out."

"They did their best." Why did he keep pushing her on this?

"It wasn't good enough." He seethed. His hands clenched at his sides, and even though he turned away from Chantal, he was so aware of her. He felt the shape of her, she barely came to his shoulder, and he felt her size, her softness, the delicacy of her features. "By staying with him, you gave him permission to hurt you—"

"I thought I could help. I thought I could change things."

"Nothing you could have done would have changed him."

"Not even if I'd been better?"

Better? he nearly cried. Better, how? How would you be better? How could you be better? "You must see it had nothing to do with you," he snapped harshly, far more harshly than he'd intended.

Chantal rubbed her bare arms, her nipples peaked beneath the thin silk fabric, obviously chilled. "I'm sorry. I didn't mean to make you angry—"

"You didn't." Guilt suffused him, endless waves of hot emotion. "I'm not angry with you. I'm angry that men hurt women. I'm angry that your husband hurt you."

"We won't talk about it anymore."

"But maybe we should talk about it. Maybe its time to get some of these secrets into the open."

"What good would it do?" She struggled to smile, attempting to be cavalier. "What's the old expression? Let by gone be bygones? Nothing we say will change the—" she broke off as he moved abruptly toward her.

Chantal took another frantic step backward. He was coming after her.

"Maybe it will change the future," he challenged. He looked positively lethal right now, his features harsh, the ridge of his prominent cheekbones jagged beneath taut bronze skin.

"You can't change the future," she protested nervously. "It hasn't even happened yet."

"So what have we been doing? Training. Preparing. Focusing.

Everything we do impacts the future. Every thought, every choice.''

He was stalking her, closing in on her, and she was sure he could see the pulse beating at the bottom of her throat, feel the fear sweeping through her, the fear a crazy combination of panic and passion. Her heart was pounding. Her stomach knotting. How did he make her feel like this? How did he create such hugely contradictory emotions?

The balcony pressed against her back. She lifted her hands, trying to soothe him. This couldn't be normal. This couldn't be the way women responded to men.

''I'm not trying to quarrel. I don't want a fight.''

''We're not fighting.''

Her legs felt like melting butter. ''You're upset.''

His dark head inclined. ''I'm a little provoked.''

A little? Maybe if she'd known more men, had more experience, she'd know how to deal with her emotions, her reactions. But she'd never known anyone like Demetrius Mantheakis, and she couldn't hide, or manage, her response to him.

He didn't stop until he was standing so close that she could see the fine weave in his shirt. Feel the heat emanate from his body. ''What's happening?'' she whispered, her heart beating so hard she thought it would burst through her chest.

''What do you think?''

Her shoulders lifted. ''I don't know. This doesn't feel right. It's...frightening.''

''What's so frightening?''

''You. This. All of this.'' Tension coiled cobralike in her. She'd never felt anything like this, never knew that this kind of energy and tension could exist between two people. The heat alone dazzled her. She felt his strength, his energy, the hard planes of his body and yet he wasn't even touching her. She wanted him.

She wanted his hands. His mouth. His body. She wanted him everywhere.

''Do *I* frighten you?''

His question forced her gaze up, her eyes meeting, locking with his.

His eyes were dark, smoky, filled with a hunger that was so physical, so raw she shivered.

He'd taken her on the beach, held her hips in his hands and driven his body into hers until she couldn't think, couldn't stop, couldn't control her little world another moment longer.

"Yes," she whispered, knowing that even as earth-shattering as the lovemaking had been, it was the aftermath which had really rocked her.

She'd loved being in his arms too much. She'd loved the seduction, the suppression of control, the intensity he stirred within her. He was far too dangerous. Far too real. She couldn't exist in his world. She'd never survive it.

"And your life?" His lips curved but it was not a friendly smile. "Does that ever frighten you?"

She didn't answer. Her mind was racing, still trying to process everything that she was thinking, feeling.

He leaned closer, his jaw hard, tight with anger. He'd shaved between breakfast and dinner and yet his jaw was already dark, and his dark eyes snapped fire. "Does it frighten you that you're like a little mouse in a cage? Absolutely trapped? Completely dominated? That everyone in your world has a say over your life...except you?"

"I'm not a mouse. I'm not trapped." But she was lying through her chattering teeth. The fact that he saw her world, her life, so clearly terrified her. Her little world, the prison that it was, was supposed to be her secret. Just like Armand's abuse was her secret shame. She couldn't discuss these things, couldn't admit such failures out loud.

"Do you have any idea how much danger you're in?" he ruthlessly persisted. "How fragile your world really is?"

She heard his voice, saw his firm lips move, but she'd shifted into panic mode. Her body was stiff, her brain freezing. She was shutting down because she didn't know how to respond.

"When are you going to confront the truth, *pedhaki mou?* You must come to grips with what your life is, and what your life isn't—"

"It's fine. My life is fine."

"It wasn't fine on the plane. On the plane you admitted you

wished you would have done things differently. You said you wished you'd fought for happiness—"

"Leave the plane out of this! That wasn't a normal conversation. That wasn't a normal night. I thought we were going to die. You got me talking and I couldn't shut up."

He smiled.

Chantal swallowed hard, skin prickling, burning. Demetrius didn't smile. Only fools smile. His voice echoed in his head, and something was making her pulse pick up, faster, faster. Too much adrenaline, she thought. Far too much emotion. She lifted a shaky hand, pushed back her hair from her temple. "That night was an anomaly. Nothing about the plane, or—" she drew a swift breath, bracing herself "—what took place on the island fits in to real life."

He cocked his head. "Not even the sex?"

The sex.

It sounded so raw that way, so physical, so heated and fierce. But then, it had been raw. And it had been hot. And she hadn't known that a man could make a woman feel like that. She hadn't known *she* could feel like that.

"Not even the sex," she answered, lifting her chin, trying desperately to prove that she, too, could be a woman of the world, and that incredible sex on a beach was something she was perfectly accustomed to.

"So you're saying that sex isn't part of your real life?"

Flushing, Chantal found herself mentally scrambling for an answer. She hadn't meant it like that, hadn't known he was going to twist her words like that. "I'm widowed."

"Surely, you've had boyfriends since Armand died."

"No."

"Dates?"

"No." She flushed yet again, her skin so hot she wished she could unzip it, cool herself off. "It's not part of my role."

"I didn't realize your role was so rigid."

"It's very…set." She purposely avoided the word rigid. "I married into a powerful monarchy and my daughter is the heir to the throne—"

"She's a little girl. You're the adult. You're entitled to have a life."

"I have a life. I adore my daughter."

"You live only for your daughter?"

"She needs me. She's four."

His dark gaze met hers, held. "What happens when she grows up?"

Frustration welled within her. Chantal didn't want to think about the distant future, couldn't even imagine the distant future. Just getting through today seemed impossible. "I don't want to talk about this anymore."

"First your husband, now your life. Is everything off limits, Princess?"

"Yes!" She shot back, furious, frustrated. He didn't respect normal boundaries, he didn't give her the space and privacy she needed. "It is to you. You were hired to protect me, not torture me, so..."

"So...?"

"Back off." But she didn't just mean verbally, or emotionally. She needed physical space, too. He was overwhelming her in every way possible. "I can't think like this. Can't breathe."

"Then breathe."

She shook her head, stunned. Not even Armand had ever spoken to her so bluntly. Pointedly. But then, Armand didn't talk. He hit. He lashed out and he lashed out when she least expected it, but Demetrius wasn't angry, he was calm. Eerily calm. He exuded control.

"I'll breathe better when you leave me alone." She drew herself as tall as she could manage considering he dwarfed her completely. Six foot one, six foot two, he was taller, broader, and stronger. He'd been built hard, rugged, built to take on the world instead of hiding from it.

"I'm not leaving you." His lashes lowered, his gaze fixed on her mouth. "And I'd never leave you alone."

"Then I'll go."

"Why?"

His voice was but a murmur of husky sound and she jerked

her head up, met his dark gaze, saw the heat in the depths, saw too late that he was as much on fire as she was.

Like the night on the beach.

Something between them burned, hot, incinerary.

Startled, aroused, she stared so long into his eyes that she lost track of time, of place, of everything she was supposed to remember.

God, no one had ever looked at her like that.

"Don't," she whispered, feeling as if she were falling even though she was still on her feet. He was leading her to the edge, she thought dizzily. He was leading her straight to disaster and she was letting it happen.

"I've done nothing." His voice was rough, and yet it brushed her senses, caressed her skin. She felt her breasts grow heavy, nipples tingling, tightening and everything she felt that night on the beach was back, everything she'd wanted was returning in waves.

Waves of longing. Waves of need.

When he looked at her like that she felt young again. When he looked at her like that she wanted to be real again. No china doll on a shelf, no pretty princess posing for the magazines.

She gave up. She leaned toward him, and even as she put herself into his space, she drew a breath. *Foolish, foolish, foolish Chantal.*

She felt his slow kiss all the way through her. It drew the air from her lungs and made her clench her fingers into fists, fighting, resisting a touch so warm, so sensual, resisting a touch that heated her so deep inside she didn't know how she'd ever put the fire out.

Better not to know you could feel this way, she told herself, reaching up to push him away and yet her hand, once pressed against his chest, couldn't let go.

Her fingers clutched at his shirt, her body drawing closer to his, curving against him as if it were the most natural place to be.

He'll ruin everything, a small voice reminded her. He'll take it all away from you. Remember what you've agreed to do. Remember your contract. Loyalty and fidelity to the Thibaudets and only the Thibaudets. She was to honor Armand's memory, up-hold his name.

The hot tears seeped from beneath her lashes and she shud-dered in his arms, a tremor of complete despair. She couldn't have passion and La Croix, and La Croix was Lilly. Lilly was home.

"You're crying." He lifted his head, stared down at her.

Chantal couldn't look away. His eyes, so dark, so intent, bored all the way through her and she felt as though he were slowly remembering it all, recalling all the words said, all the things done, all the emotion surging through her now. "This is a cruel twist of fate."

Frowning, he wiped away tears from her cheek. "How so?"

She grew hot, cold, and hot all over again, and unable to speak, she leaned against him, feeling his strength, the shape of his chest a curve of smooth dense muscle that invited further exploration. "You're not part of my world. You're not what I can have."

His narrowed gaze took in the wetness of her tears, the softness of her mouth. "What can you have?"

"Nothing." The word was wrenched from her.

"And you accept these limitations?"

Her lips curved in a hard, brittle smile. "I don't have a choice."

"Everyone has a choice."

"Not me." Sanity was returning, little by little, awareness of her, of him, of the restrictions placed on her. She had to stop this madness before she lost reason completely. This wasn't love. It was lust. This wasn't right. It was a product of nerves, of hormones, of imagination.

But Demetrius didn't like her answer, and he wasn't going to accept it, either. He dropped his hands from her face to lightly encircle her waist. His touch was so hot, so electric she felt as if he'd singed her. "And you really believe that?"

She loved the way his hands felt on her, loved the pressure, the touch, the connection between them, and yet when she looked into his eyes she saw a fierceness...a rage...that knocked the wind from her.

His hand rose, stroked her high on her side, over her ribs to cup her breast.

She shivered. *"Demetrius."*

He drew her even closer, and the feel of his palm curving against her full, sensitive breast made her head spin.

This was the way a man should hold a woman. This was the way she'd always wanted to be held. Firmly. Securely. Nothing tentative about it at all.

For a split-second Chantal could imagine a life like this, a life safe in the Greek's arms, his body between her and the world, his shoulders shielding her from the press, his strength holding her up when she didn't think she could smile one more smile, pose for one more photograph. His body taking her body late at night, taking her places no one else could ever take her...

His lips covered hers again, and when his mouth parted hers, she dug her fingers into his shirt again, fabric balled in her palm and she prayed for strength.

Remember your position. Remember your situation. If nothing else, for God's sake, remember Lilly. If you can think of nothing else, think of her.

And focusing, remembering, she pushed away. It took every ounce of strength to walk away from him, but she did. She backed up, one step, two steps, until she found herself half way across the room, staring at him as if he were a mirage, something conjured from her own imagination.

"You're letting them own you, Chantal."

She shook her head, stunned by the emptiness inside her. She felt as if he'd ripped her insides wide-open and let in the warm night air. The emptiness—the massive gaping hole—horrified her. "What have you done to me?"

"It's all you, *pedhaki mou.*"

She swayed, felt the delicate beaded silk fabric of her dress brush the back of her legs. "This isn't me. This isn't who I am."

"And you said sex wasn't part of your real life." He made a rough sound, mocking, impatient. "Maybe it should be. You're a woman that was born to be loved."

Chantal lifted a hand in protest and the glint of her wedding ring caught her eye. She balled her hand, feeling the press of the sapphire against her skin. Her stomach heaved.

What a nightmare. It had all become an endless dreadful dream.

Phillipe and Catherine Thibaudet, Armand's parents, had insisted she continue wearing the ring, just as they'd insisted she continue as it'd been before Armand died. And it had to be that way. It's what she'd agreed to all those years ago. It's the deal she'd made.

God forgive her for signing contracts she didn't understand.

"Don't kiss me again," she said, trying to look taller, stronger than she felt. "Promise me you won't ever kiss—touch me—again."

"Can't."

"Can't?"

"Won't," he corrected. "I don't make promises I won't keep."

CHAPTER NINE

HIS answer took her breath away. She burned all the way through—her heart, chest, body on fire. The noise in her head was so loud it was like a thousand helicopters buzzing.

"You're intentionally making this difficult," she said, her voice coming out hoarse, raw.

"No. I'm just being honest. I could never make that promise, Princess. Not in a thousand years." He caught her by the arm, his hand easily encircling her slender bicep. "But I promise to be true to you. And I'll promise to be with you no matter what, that I shall face every danger with you—"

"Why? I'm nothing but a job to you!"

His features shifted. "But you're a job I like."

The anger and passion in his voice left her reeling, and she shook her head, bewildered. Once more she tried to pull away, and this time he let her go.

She walked away from him, moving across the room to look out the window. The sky outside had grown dark and household staff were silently moving through the terraces lighting fat golden candles, which threw off soft rays of light.

One of the maids stepped into the living room. "Dinner," the maid said, bowing slightly.

Chantal took her seat at the table in the dining room. The long wooden table had been draped with a pure white lace cloth, a half dozen tall white candles softening the stark room with soft yellow light. The dining room boasted a massive plated window with a breathtaking view of the water, which had begun to reflect the moonlight.

But all the moonlight in the world couldn't ease her internal chaos. She felt so exposed sitting there with the lights dimmed, Demetrius's face alternately lit and shadowed by flickering candlelight.

Her dress was delicate, barely there, and yet she felt so hot.

Her skin burned. Her stomach clenched. She couldn't even bring herself to look at Demetrius. How was it possible to want someone so badly?

"You didn't eat much," he said, as the dinner dishes were cleared.

He was right. She couldn't eat much. Even though she felt empty and restless, her hunger had nothing to do with food, and everything to do with touch. Pleasure. Sensation. "Not much of an appetite," she answered, staring at the skewered bite of broiled lamb sitting on her plate.

"I can have the cook prepare something different."

"No. I like lamb."

"Just not this lamb?"

It's not the lamb, she wanted to snap, her fingers tightening, flexing in her lap, her body humming with a nervous, restless energy. She hated the heat in her face, the hunger in her heart, the memory of how it'd been between them. If the sex had been bad, or her body indifferent, she wouldn't be feeling this way. But the night they'd shared on Sao Tome had been stunning and the sex unreal. Everything that had happened between them had been...so not ordinary, and it was that sense of the extraordinary which had swept her up, made her feel, made her imagine that maybe, just maybe, there was more for her, maybe...

"I'm okay. Really." She managed a small tight smile. And it struck her that what she wanted wasn't sex...or a body...it wasn't even a man. She wanted *him*. Demetrius Mantheakis. The hard, tough Greek. But she didn't understand the attraction, didn't know what it was about him that made her pulse race, her imagination fly.

What in God's name was wrong with her? How could she be so pathetic? She'd lived right for years. She'd made the choices she was supposed to make and she'd said yes, Your Highness, no, Your Highness, anything else Your Highness?

"Dessert? Fruit and cheese?" he offered.

She dug her nails into her hands. He was worrying about the fact that she'd sent her plate back to the kitchen virtually untouched while she was going mad with desire. She didn't want food. She wanted *him*.

She wanted him to unzip her dress and slide his bare hands across her back, down to her hips, around her thighs.

She wanted the darkest room, the softest bed, seductive silence.

Instead she touched her neck, wrapped her fingers around her warm skin, feeling far too tense, impossibly sensitive. She touched the very place she wanted his hands, imagined how his lips would feel, not just on her neck, but on her breast, on her tight nipple.

Eyes briefly closing, she could feel the heat rise in her, the yearning so strong she felt as if she was dissolving. "Would you mind if I turned in early?" She asked, struggling to hide the flare of need. She couldn't continue to sit here, across from him, couldn't stand feeling so bare and raw.

His eyes met hers and held. "Yes. I want you to take a look at something first. You can either wait here while I get the information, or you can join me in my office."

"What information?" she asked, shooting him a mistrustful glance. His features were even, his expression perfectly controlled and yet she felt his brooding silence, a stillness in him that reminded her of a hawk perched high above, watchful. Waiting.

"Just come with me. You'll see."

She followed him downstairs to his office suite. It was more elaborate than she'd thought—two interconnecting offices and a separate conference room. He led her to the conference room where papers were spread across the table.

He picked up most of the papers but left a couple on the table. "Have a look at this," he said, pushing several pages toward her.

She glanced down at the papers he'd given her. They were letters. Handwritten. Addressed to her. On one page the handwriting was small, narrow, tightly contained. On the other page the handwriting was bigger, looser, an uncontrollable scrawl. "These letters are to me."

"Yes." He leaned forward, watched her skim one and then the next. "I've kept the worst of the letters from you. But I hoped that you'd recognize the handwriting."

''No.'' She looked up at him. ''I'm sorry. I wish I did.''

Demetrius sighed. ''I didn't think you would, but it was worth the chance.'' He took the letters back from her, glanced down at the page with the wild scrawl. ''The letters were mailed to the palace in Melio, but they're postmarked from La Croix, from the main post office near the Thibaudet châteaux.''

It was a struggle to concentrate when he looked at her so intently. ''So the danger is in La Croix. And it could be someone at the châteaux.''

He nodded. ''We're having the handwriting analyzed, but the detectives working the case are certain it's a man, and someone fairly educated.''

''Hard to believe I could have such an obsessive...fan.'' She felt fear spread through her. ''I've tried to live simply. Quietly.''

''Obviously not quietly enough. Someone's noticed you, and someone wants you.''

Dead, she silently finished, trying to control her pulse, her heart now beating a little faster. And Tanguy had already paid a horrible price for someone's sick obsession. ''Any ideas about this person's lifestyle or occupation?''

''Not at the moment.''

''But there must be some kind of profile—''

''There is. But, unfortunately, these guys don't wear their profiles on their sleeve. The stalker is a predator. They hide their intentions, work hard to appear normal.'' His brows lowered. ''Most think they're normal.''

Demetrius saw her pale. He didn't want to upset her, but he needed her cooperation. They had to apprehend the stalker before the stalker hurt anyone else.

Demetrius's firm had dealt with fan obsession before—many times before. Of all the forms of security work, this was his least favorite. Not because it wasn't vital, but because it was such unpredictable work. The stalker was one of the hardest, most difficult threats to control because he could be anyone, could blend in anywhere, could hide in a crowd, could slip in, out, silent, secret, unnoticed.

''Why do you do this?'' she asked, her voice shaking a little.

"It's so..." She suddenly shivered. She didn't bother to finish her sentence.

"Sordid," he supplied, his lips twisting. "But that's what I like. What I do—what my firm does—helps people. I'm glad I can help and protect people, because I know what its like to lose sleep when someone you love is in danger. I know its impossible to eat when your insides are sick with fear. I lived that way for three weeks once, and it was the longest three weeks in my life."

His voice was hard, his tone dark. She felt a shiver race through her. "I hope your story has a happy ending."

His features seemed to freeze. His expression turned ruthless. "No."

She felt a chill race through her. Something horrible had happened in his life and the tragedy had made him the man she saw now, the man who refused to let her cower or hide. "How did you survive your loss?"

"Revenge."

She didn't like this conversation, didn't want to imagine how Demetrius had suffered, much less how he might have made another suffer. "Do you...do...that sort of thing today?"

"No. I play by the book now."

"I see."

"You don't approve."

She tried to smile. "I don't like pain."

"No. You'd rather go through life pretending happiness, wearing that lovely royal mask and letting the world think you're beautiful inside and out."

He knew how to hurt her too well. "You are awfully dangerous, aren't you?"

"You're more dangerous. You're dying on the inside and you won't even admit it. I, at least, want to help you."

She stared at him from across the table, air trapped so long inside her lungs that little specks appeared before her eyes. He was right. She hated him for being right. Anger bubbled up in her, resentment that he always seemed to have the answer. "Did it ever cross your mind that I don't want your help? That I've accepted my life—"

"Bullshit."

Her cheeks colored. "Excuse me?"

"Let's not do this, Chantal. We don't have to do this. It was sex. It was nothing more than sex. Let's just keep it at that, okay?" And dropping the letters back on the table, Demetrius headed for the door. "You know your way back to your room, so I'll let you stay and poke around my office if you'd like. But I'm heading upstairs. I need some air. Good night."

He walked out.

She watched him and something in her chest squeezed, vise-like. Tears stung her eyes. It wasn't supposed to be like this.

Inside her room she undressed slowly, removing her dress for her nightgown, and she felt as if she were moving in slow motion.

She'd married Armand because Melio was bankrupt, and she, intellectual that she was, understood that duty came first. That duty would always come first.

But God forgive her, she hated duty. Hated everything about duty. Yet it was too late. She couldn't stop what she'd started. Couldn't escape what she'd agreed to do.

Moving to her bedroom window, Chantal pressed her face to the slick pane, needing the coolness of the glass to soothe her hot skin. She felt wild inside. Tangled. Angry.

And standing at the window, she spotted him below, out on the pool terrace. Her heart pounded. Her thoughts went wild. She wanted to go to him, or send for him. But if she did, what then?

What then indeed?

The loneliness was unbearable, and turning from the window, Chantal leaned against the wall, closed her eyes, her hand sliding inside her robe to cover her chest.

Her skin felt so tender and smooth, warm, warm with the curve of her breast beneath her palm and her even softer silkier nipple against her fingertips. She felt touchable, needing to be touchable, needed to be touched and held and loved.

Her hand slid slowly from her breast, down the middle of her rib cage to her flat abdomen, muscles tensing, nerve endings stirring. She could imagine his hand touching her like this, could imagine the sensation and knew she'd like being with him, knew she'd welcome every touch, every kiss, every caress.

Madness.

Abruptly she drew her hand from her robe and pulled the edges of it together, trying. What are you going to do Chantal? If you make love to him again, you're going to fall in love. You're going to fall so hard you'll never be able to get out in one piece.

She tugged the wood shutters closed, blocking out the mysterious night with the high white moon and the sprinkle of faraway stars.

The silk coverlet on her bed had already been folded back, the cool cotton sheets exposed, and Chantal pulled the top sheet back feeling more alone than she had in years.

A knock sounded on her door before she could climb between the sheets.

She crossed the room, opened the door. Her heart slowed, stopped, the air strangled in her throat. "Demetrius."

He didn't say a word. He just stood there, looking at her, frustration etched deeply in his hard features.

He was still wearing his dark trousers but his shirt hung open, revealing his bare chest. His thick dark hair stood on end as if he'd spent the last ten minutes dragging his fingers through it.

She couldn't tear her gaze from his face. He looked as if he were absolutely tortured. Heart thudding, she opened her door wider and watched his dark eyes grow hotter, the brown depths smoldering, like volcanic rock pulled from fire.

She touched the tip of her tongue to the inside of her bottom lip. Her lip felt fat, heavy, swollen. Her body felt just as heavy. "Do you want to come in?"

"You know what will happen if I do."

Silently she stepped back, drawing the door wider still, and with her breath bottled inside her, she watched him enter her bedroom. He walked slowly around the room, measured steps that matched his close measured gaze. He was looking at everything, taking in every detail, locking it away in his incredible brain.

He sat down on the edge of the bed and looked at her. She felt her legs tremble. "Come to me," he said, and liquid silver raced through her, turning her into endless need.

She went to him and he parted his thighs and pulled her between them. She felt his thighs close, trap her between his legs, his knees on either side of her hips. He was strong. The muscles of his thighs held her firmly, his hands settled on her waist and his fingers burned through her pale peach silk nightgown.

"This is just sex, right?" he demanded harshly.

Her eyes burned and she struggled to smile. "It couldn't be anything else."

A tiny muscle pulled in his jaw, tightening his mouth but he said nothing.

His silence said more than words ever could and she flushed deeply, looked at him, looked away.

He caught her hair in his fist, turned her face back to his. His dark brown eyes held a mixture of pain and anger. "So it is just sex you want."

She didn't understand what he wanted her to say, didn't understand where he hoped this would go. He knew her world. He knew her commitments. He knew what she had to do. "Yes."

The corner of his mouth curved. "Fine." He reached up to cup her breast even before his lips covered hers.

His kiss burned her. His kiss was hard and demanding, his kiss, like the hand on her breast, spoke of ownership. Possession. But he didn't stop there. Clasping her face between his hands, he turned her into a captive and there was no escaping the insistent pressure of his mouth now. His lips were firm, and he explored her mouth with his tongue, tasting her, filling her, heightening sensation until she whimpered for more.

Blindly Chantal reached for him, hands settling on his chest, fingers twining in his shirt as she struggled to meet her need for more contact, more pleasure.

This was raw, she thought wildly, this was fierce and hot and he made her want to strip off her clothes and cool off—or to just drag him over her and have him fill her, really fill her and give her relief.

Funny, but her need for him, physically seemed to come from something deeper, leaping to life from an emotional well inside of her. She'd felt numb for so many years and the numbness was gone, to be replaced by an inferno of desire. For one crazy second she vowed she'd give up everything just to answer the need. Just to satisfy the craving.

He lifted her into his arms, carried her around to the side of the bed, and when he set her on the mattress, he immediately followed, his big body moving over hers, parting her thighs.

Lifting the hem of her nightgown, he impatiently tugged it over her head, and his hands replaced her gown, covering her breasts, touching her hips, molding the softness of her belly.

She felt him caress her hip, the inside of her thigh and then he was touching her there, at the apex of her thighs, his fingertips brushing the dark curls and then between, finding her silken and warm, finding each taut nerve ending.

She gasped softly as he parted her inner lips, and stroked her, once, and again, from the delicate peaked nub down, across the burning tender skin to the tantalizing opening that was craving to be filled by him. The lightness of his touch, the sureness of his touch, made her tense and grasp the coverlet between her hands. She was melting in her need, and as his fingers dipped into her, filling her, she felt herself dissolve, becoming hotter, wetter, her body hungering for him.

"Make love to me," she said, reaching up to encircle his neck with her arms. She drew him down to her. "I've never wanted anyone, or anything, like I want this."

"The sex is that good?" His eyes creased but his voice sounded hard, cynical.

Tears burned the back of her eyes. "You're that good." *I could love you, you know. I could love you forever.*

She closed her eyes as his lips covered hers in another hard, possessive kiss. She felt his body press against hers, felt his hair roughened chest, felt his hard flat abdomen, felt the ridge in his trousers.

Chantal slid a hand down his stomach, fingers groping for the button on his trousers. If she couldn't have forever, she thought, she'd at least have this.

They made love twice—intense, demanding, incredibly erotic sex—and after she climaxed the second time, she curled up in his arms, skin still damp, body still shuddering, and she felt his strong arms wrap around her, holding her securely to him.

She'd never felt so loved in all her life.

But this isn't love, she told herself, this was sex.

Liar.

"You—this—amazes me," she said softly, struggling to find the words even as her palm pressed against his chest, his heart beating beneath her hand. "It's incredible. Being here with you. Like this."

He didn't speak, and she felt his silence all the way through her.

"I won't ever forget it," she added, wanting him to say something. Maybe even to agree. Yes, Chantal, this is wonderful. No, Chantal, I'll never forget you...

But he didn't say a word. He wasn't agreeing. He wasn't conceding. He wasn't going to let her have her way.

"I won't forget you," she added, stomach muscles tightening. "You've...meant...a lot to me."

"It was sex," he corrected almost cruelly. "Remember?"

"Because it has to be." She swallowed, felt pain radiate out through her, replacing the warmth, erasing the pleasure. "This life I have isn't what I want, it's not what I ever dreamed it'd be—"

"So break away."

She gathered the thirty years of hard training into her shaking limbs and rolled away from him, to sit up, her arms encircling her legs. "You don't understand."

"Try me."

"I can't. It's too complicated, too unbelievable to explain."

"Try me," he repeated stubbornly.

The resolve in his voice sent shivers through her. "It's rather dry, actually. Facts and figures, not fun and romance."

He barked a laugh. "I studied economics at university, Princess. I'm sure I can handle the dry details."

"Maybe you will find this interesting then." Her arms tightened around her bent legs, even as she struggled to organize her thoughts, simplify the story into one concise paragraph. "You know that my marriage was an arranged marriage. But most people don't. The magazines never printed anything about it being arranged, and from the lavish wedding no one would guess that the Ducasse-Thibaudet marriage was really about two countries brokering a deal.''

She shot him a glance, and even in the dark saw the grim set of his mouth. Swallowing, she pushed on. ''As you can expect with any important deal, there was lots of paperwork attached, clauses and contracts, plus a wordy pre-nuptial. I never imagined I'd be widowed so young, just as I never imagined my marriage would be so miserable, so I agreed to the terms that seem ludicrous now. But Melio benefited. La Croix provided my country with financial aid. Everyone seemed happy.''

''Except you.''

Her shoulders lifted and fell. ''In any merger or takeover there's bound to be some hurt feelings.''

His jaw tightened and he shook his head once, a short angry shake. ''But this is more than hurt feelings, this is slavery, Princess.''

That was putting it bluntly, she thought, her eyes prickling in the dark. But she managed a brittle smile, a hint of her old bravado. Once she'd been so brave. Once she honestly thought she could do anything.

''Shh,'' she whispered, trying to tease, but her voice broke. ''It's our dirty little secret.''

His arm reached out for her, and he pulled her back down onto the mattress. ''Dirty is the word I'd use.''

He rolled her over, trapping her beneath him. His head descended, his lips covering hers, taking her, and her heart felt as if it would explode.

She loved being with him. She loved being kissed by him. If only this could be real, if only this were part of her world...

He deepened the kiss and she felt herself melt, heart, body, limbs, opening for him, needing him and he knew. He parted her knees, making room for his warm hard body between her thighs.

She shuddered as the rigid length of him pressed against her still damp, sensitized core. He belonged here, with her, she thought, reaching for him, wrapping her arms around his neck. And slowly he entered her, in a long smooth thrust that felt like warm silk sliding on warmer satin. She cried out against his mouth, and his lips caught the sound, held it in him, between them, and being taken like this, filled like this, filled the emptiest part of her mind, never mind what he was doing to her body.

Emotion wrapped around her heart, tight and tighter. Chantal released his shoulders, hands sliding down the back of his thick triceps, to his elbows, then his hips. She felt the powerful muscles in his hips clench, felt his buttocks knot as he buried himself even deeper.

The pressure, the pleasure, it was all so intense and the sensation he created with his body against hers made her want to give him everything, if only for this night.

Because no one had ever loved her this way. No one had ever held her this way. No one had ever kissed her mouth with such tenderness and hunger, passion and need. No one had ever made her feel so feminine and beautiful, and yet intelligent and capable. He was everything she couldn't have and yet right now, he was everything she needed.

Everything she wanted.

I love you, she thought, twin rings of emotion wrapping around her heart. She did love him. She knew now it wasn't lust, wasn't a passing fancy. She also knew that back in La Croix she'd never be able to be with him like this. In La Croix she'd never see him.

Demetrius suddenly shifted his weight, reached around for her ankle. "Wrap your legs around me," he urged, his voice deep, dark, full of passion. "Higher."

She did as he told her, and as she moved beneath him, he kissed her exposed neck and was rewarded with a shiver. She felt his lips curve against her warm skin and he slipped his hands beneath her hips, tilting her even more. "Better?" he asked.

Oh, she was completely his now. "Yes."

"Then hang on," he said with the rough male voice that made her tingle all the way through, "and don't let go."

CHAPTER TEN

CHANTAL woke, and even before she reached out, she knew Demetrius was gone.

And it devastated her. She didn't want him gone. Didn't want to wake up alone. But this is real life, she reminded herself. This is the way its going to be.

She sat up. Her stomach heaved. A violent heave that made her mouth taste funny, all silver metallic tasting.

Slowly she lay down again, placed a hand on her stomach, trying to calm it down. This wasn't a hang over. She didn't even touch her wine last night. Was it food poisoning maybe?

After a few minutes she forced herself up again, dragging herself into a sitting position, giving herself a chance to fight the queasiness, and as she sat there, she felt a whisper of warmth. Demetrius. Demetrius Mantheakis. Darkly handsome. Her sexy, brooding Greek.

Last night had been unreal. By far the most beautiful night of her life. Every moment in his arms was perfect. And yet that kind of emotion, that intensity of feeling, only made everything else pale in comparison.

Don't think about him. Don't think at all. Just get up. Get moving. The night's over. You have to get on with your life.

Pushing off the bed, Chantal did her best to ignore her queasy stomach as she took a bath and dressed before heading downstairs for breakfast.

She stepped out onto the terrace surfaced in buffed limestone. The creamy stones reflected the warm morning sun, and the bright clear sunlight dazzled her, making her head spin.

Where was Demetrius now? What was he doing? She wanted to see him. She was afraid to see him. Yet he was nowhere in sight this morning as she seated herself on the terrace.

The day was already gorgeous, and it had to do with the quality of the light. The air here was luminous—bright, clear, and it glazed the whitewashed walls of the house and garden, shimmered off the green and blue ocean, dappled her table with the bowl of fresh cut fruit.

The breakfast of tea and toast settled her stomach and Chantal was just about to leave the table when Demetrius appeared.

Even though they'd spent the night together, just seeing him this morning sent shock waves through her. God, he was big. Strong. So darkly beautiful.

She swallowed the rush of emotion—love and pain washing through her in fierce waves.

His eyes met hers and for a split-second she imagined she saw the same emotion there in his dark gaze. Her heart ached as she stared up at him. *I love you. I want you. I don't get to keep you, do I?*

A muscle in his jaw pulled, and then his features relaxed, tension disappearing and his expression was impassive...almost bored. "Finished?" he asked, indicating her meal.

No hello, darling. No tender good morning. Nothing to indicate that anything special had passed between them last night.

To hide the intensity of her disappointment she forced a cool smile. "Yes, thank you."

He was wearing denim shorts and a black T-shirt with cutoff sleeves. "Ready?" he asked.

She'd never seen him so casual and her narrowed gaze swept his long muscular legs, the thickly muscled arms, his skin darkly bronzed. "Where are we going?"

"I thought you could use a change of scenery, so we're going to head out. Spend the day on my boat."

It wasn't, she thought later, the best idea, not when her body felt so achy and tired. Her stomach didn't help, either, not with it churning so wildly, but she somehow managed to make it through the afternoon without giving her discomfort away. But in the end, it wasn't her queasy stomach that undid her. It was Demetrius's distance. She'd secretly hoped that on the boat he might be more personal, less aloof. Instead he was the consummate professional. He was near her, but never touched her. He was polite, but not conversational. He was watchful, but detached.

And it was awful. His distance made her feel awful, and instead of enjoying the sail back to the Rock, she seethed inwardly, emotions fierce, wild, nearly impossible to control.

How could he make love to her at night and keep her at arm's length during the day?

Maybe it was the lovemaking from the night before, the day spent on the boat, or the hours in the sun, but whatever it was, on returning to the villa Chantal felt absolutely exhausted.

She couldn't remember when she last felt so tired, and heading upstairs, she closed the wood shutters at the windows, darkening her room. After stripping off her clothes, leaving just her underwear, she climbed into bed between soft cool white sheets.

Dinner that evening was an agony.

It wasn't just Demetrius's company fraying her nerves, it was her body itself. Her body had ceased to cooperate. From the moment she entered the dining room her stomach rebelled.

The very smell of poached fish curdled her stomach, and Chantal took a step back, nearly covering her mouth and nose, fighting the wave of nausea. She hadn't felt all that well today but the fish…no way. She couldn't do it.

Demetrius caught her gaze. His eyebrow lifted.

She returned to her chair, shook her head, forcing a brief smile. Nothing was wrong, she said with her smile. Nothing could ever be wrong.

But sitting down, she felt her stomach do another threatening cramp and fine beads of moisture broke out on her brow and upper lip. She'd been tired and achy all day. She couldn't have the flu again, could she?

Just get through dinner, she told herself, and then go back to your room and back to bed.

But getting through dinner wasn't going to be easy. Her stomach was churning and her body felt so hot and cold she could barely get her water glass to her lips without her hand trembling like mad. Exhausted by the effort to just sit at the table and take the odd sip of soup, she didn't even try to make conversation and Demetrius didn't try to encourage her to speak, either. But he was watching her. Closely. With that unnerving intensity which always made her feel as if she were a science experiment beneath a microscope.

Chantal managed to swallow another tiny mouthful of the spicy fish chowder even though her stomach protested nonstop. She didn't know how much longer she was going to be able to sit here and pretend everything was okay. She didn't feel okay. She felt…sick.

Abruptly Demetrius leaned forward and pressed the back of his hand to her forehead. "What's wrong?"

Her instinctive response was to answer nothing. But her body was overruling her head. She couldn't lie. She was going to throw up—soon. "I need to go to my room."

"What's wrong?" he repeated, rising even as she did.

"I don't know." She wouldn't meet his eyes. She couldn't let him see just how sick she was feeling. Being ill was personal. Private. And worse, throwing up was so undignified. She hated being undignified. "If you'll excuse me—"

"I'm coming with you."

"No."

But he already had a hand wrapped under her upperarm and he was half leading, half dragging her away from the courtyard table back to her bedchamber on the second floor.

Halfway up the staircase her face burned even as the rest of her went cold and clammy. She put a hand out, pushed blindly against him. "Demi—"

He understood, sweeping her into his arms and dashing up the rest of the stairs. She was ill before they reached the bathroom.

Tears burned her eyes, nearly as bitter as the bile in her mouth. In the bathroom he placed her on the edge of the massive bathtub. "I'm sorry," she choked, accepting the damp wash towel he handed her.

"Doesn't matter," he said. "It's nothing." All cold and trembly, she blotted her mouth and forced herself to look at him.

His shoulder was covered.

She closed her eyes, horrified, ashamed. She shouldn't have. Armand would have never forgiven her.

Forcing herself to action, she stood, cleared her throat, even though her stomach was rumbling again. "Let me have your shirt."

"We have staff to do our laundry," he answered, and again he reached out to touch her face, this time her cheek. "When did this first hit you?"

"I haven't felt well much of the day. But I thought it was just fatigue. The walk up and down the hill. The sun." She shrugged. "It's probably just a touch of something," she said, wishing he'd get rid of that shirt, wishing he'd go back to his room, wishing to just escape his hard watchful gaze that suggested both suspicion and danger.

"What?"

"Flu bug," she answered.

His jaw tightened. His eyes narrowed. "Or maybe a touch of food poisoning," she added, uncomfortably.

"We've eaten the same food," he answered.

He trusted no one, she thought, stifling a rather hysterical laugh. Not even her.

"Well, I can assure you I'm not poisoning myself." She placed a hand across her stomach now heaving. She could feel the muscles dance on the insides, tiny pulsating ripples.

Oh, no. Not again. She was going to be sick soon. Too soon.

"You better go," she choked, grateful she was sitting, knowing her legs wouldn't support her now. But even though she sat, she felt so weak she just wanted to slide down, a slow boneless slide to the floor where she could press her hot cheek to the cold white marble surrounding the toilet.

"You're going to be sick again, aren't you?" But he didn't even wait for her to answer. He was already pulling her up, positioning her before the toilet, his arms holding her securely, far too firmly.

Shivering, Chantal felt small and helpless and she hated it. "Please go."

"I'm not leaving you now, Princess."

She didn't miss the grimness in his voice. Why did he insist on calling her princess at the most inappropriate moments? The times she wanted the civility he refused to give it to her, and then when she felt so humble, so ordinary he had to stick her title in her face. "But I don't want you here," she panted, stomach roiling, skin damp, her whole body rebelling. "You're not needed here. This is something I can do on my own."

And before she could utter another word, she was clutching the sides of the porcelain toilet, sick, sicker, and surprisingly grateful when she was finally finished that Demetrius was there to hand her another damp towel and help her strip her dirty blouse off and start the bath.

With the bath quickly filling, he gathered the soiled towels and her blouse and glanced at her where she perched on the closed toilet seat. "I'll go," he said. "But I'm going to be back." He hesitated, inspecting her pale clammy face. "And don't lock the door. I'd hate to break a good door down just to get to you."

"But you would."

"Of course I would."

She gazed up at him through bleary eyes, her hair damp and stringy against her cheek. She felt like hell. Please let this just be a twenty-four hour flu. "Can I just tell you again that you're not a normal bodyguard?"

She was surprised to see a flash of humor in his eyes.

"Good. I've spent my whole life trying to be anything but normal." He nodded. "I'll see you in a few minutes."

Fortunately he gave her ten blissfully undisturbed minutes and by the time he returned she'd already wrapped herself in a plush robe and slipped between her cool cotton bedsheets.

He knocked on her door and entered without waiting for permission, carrying a small woven tray the color of burnt caramel. "Crackers and ginger ale," he said, setting the tray in easy arm's reach on her nightstand. He looked pleased to see her already in bed.

She glanced at the woven tray. Tiny bubbles fizzed in the ginger ale. "Thank you. That's very kind of you."

He gestured impatiently. "It's what any decent human being would do."

"Then thank you for being decent."

The next day, late afternoon, Demetrius walked into her bathroom where she was crouching next to the toilet and dropped a pink and white box on the counter. The writing on the box was in Greek and English.

A home pregnancy test kit.

She swallowed, looked at the box and then up at Demetrius. As usual, his expression was shuttered and impossible to read. But obviously something was on his mind.

"It's not food poisoning," he said, breaking the taut silence. "And it's not the flu."

"You can't be sure."

"Take the test." His deep voice echoed off the polished marble.

"I'm not pregnant." She forced herself up, from the floor of the bathroom to sit on the closed toilet seat. She'd spent more time in the bathroom today then she'd spent in the last six months. "I'd know if I was pregnant—"

"You have morning sickness."

"Afternoon sickness," she corrected, willing herself not to look at the box on the counter, willing him to be wrong even though she knew he was probably right. "I didn't feel this way with Lilly."

"The doctor said every pregnancy is different."

She felt her eyebrows arch even as heat flooded her cheeks. "You consulted the doctor about me?"

"I consulted a physician about my wife's pregnancy." His words were clipped, like splinters of ice. "She had a very difficulty pregnancy. She was sick like this—day and night."

Chantal felt the heat give way to something altogether different. Fingers curling into her palms, she suppressed the wave off emotion rolling through her, working just as hard at resisting the impulse to ask him what happened to this wife and child. Where did she go? Where is your child now?

But even without asking the questions, she saw the answers in his face. His eyes said it all.

The wife was gone. The child was gone. He'd been alone on his own a long time.

Mutely she rose, reached for the pregnancy kit. "How long does it take to get the results?"

"A couple minutes."

She nodded, numb, overwhelmed, resigned. She didn't want to know the truth. She didn't want to see proof when she'd worked so hard to ignore the facts staring herself in the face.

They'd had unprotected sex over two and a half weeks ago. Her breasts were tender. Her emotions were volatile. And she was sick, sick, sick to her stomach. Like the flu, but worse, because this could last for months. Nine months, specifically.

Holding her breath, she opened the box, slid out the foil pouch with the individual test kit. The tester felt so slender, so medicinal. With trembling fingers she opened the pouch. ''I'll let you know.''

''I'll be waiting.''

A minute and a half later the unknown was known. It didn't even take two full minutes. Yes, she was pregnant. Two dark pink lines. Positive.

Opening the bathroom door, she saw Demetrius sitting in a chair by the window. The sunlight poured through the window, illuminating his head and shoulders.

He stood when she opened the door. His eyes met hers. Unable to find her voice, she nodded.

For a heartbeat he did nothing, then he, too nodded. And then he left.

That was it. Nothing had been said, and yet everything had been said. There were moments when words were utterly unnecessary.

Yet just because they didn't speak that afternoon or evening about Chantal's condition, it didn't mean Demetrius was indifferent. It took him hours to fall asleep, and when he did, his dreams were all nightmares, one unending nightmare that clawed at him, holding him transfixed.

Katina in the hands of the enemy, pregnant and terrified. He felt Katina's fear. He saw the terror in her eyes. She didn't understand what was happening, why it was happening, and all she could think about was protecting the baby.

The baby.

In the dream he saw her put a hand up to her swollen belly, the baby's birth just seven weeks away, soothing the baby, reassuring the baby, trying desperately to reassure herself.

In the dream he stretched out an arm to grab her and then the ground opened, swallowed her whole.

In the dream he threw himself at the earth and tried to keep the ground from closing. *Katina!*

Demetrius woke in a cold sweat. He sat up, tossed the covers aside, and headed for the bathroom where he drenched his clammy face with handfuls of cold water.

He hadn't had the dreams in years. He hadn't felt this kind of nameless terror since he bought the Rock. The Rock had given him a sanctuary but Chantal's pregnancy stripped the illusion away.

The pregnancy, he thought, opening the French doors leading to his balcony, changed everything.

His mission had changed. It was no longer a job about protecting a princess, but a job about protecting the mother of his child.

Demetrius's head swam, a dizzying rush of reality and emotion. He couldn't believe it. She was pregnant. This shouldn't have happened but it had.

Leaning against the balcony, he gulped in the cool night air. He'd never thought he'd have another chance. Never thought he'd father another child. He'd been so careful in all his relationships to ensure his lover was protected, that there could be no mistake—that there would be no mistake. His women knew straight off the bat that he wasn't interested in marriage, family, or commitment. He'd had his one family, the only family he'd ever wanted to have, and he'd had no desire to replace what he'd lost. Replacing Katina and the baby seemed cruel. People couldn't be replaced. His wife's tragic death so close to their baby's due date had turned him inside out, taken his mind and shaved it in two. Heartbroken, discipline gone, he'd set out to avenge Katina and their baby daughter's death, and he had.

He had.

He'd done what a good, God-fearing man wouldn't do.

He'd fully expected the Family would answer his vengeance with a retaliation of their own. And he'd been almost disappointed when it didn't come. Truthfully, death would have been easier than life. Truthfully, dying and joining Katina and the baby would have at least given him peace. But peace wasn't forthcoming.

The Family left him alone. The Family let him go.

And that, had been the end of Demetrius Manthakeis, loving father, protective family man.

But now it'd all changed again. Now, somehow, rather miraculously, it seemed, he'd be a father again.

If the princess didn't terminate the pregnancy.

If the stalker didn't terminate the princess.

Exhaling in a slow, hard rush of air, Demetrius stared out at the dark sea, seeing just one small light out on the endless expanse of water. One little boat, he thought, in all that water.

One little life inside Chantal. A life he knew he'd protect with his own.

He joined Chantal as soon as he saw her appear on the terrace for breakfast. "We need to talk."

Her expression wary, she slowly sat down at the table. He was grateful she didn't say anything stupid like *What do we need to talk about?* There was so much unspoken between them, so much heaviness, and silence. He had to know what she was thinking...planning...had to get a sense of what was going on right now inside her head.

"How did you sleep?" he asked, accepting a coffee from the silent housekeeper who appeared and disappeared before anyone could acknowledge her.

Chantal's head tipped, her hair in a glossy brown ponytail. "Not well."

"I didn't, either." The best thing to do was come out and say what was on his mind. "All I did last night was think. Think about you. The baby—"

"Hardly a baby, yet."

His brows furrowed and he was tempted to say something sharp when her head lifted and she met his gaze. Her expression was sober, intense, her blue eyes dark with a night spent soul searching. She was trying to make sense of this just as he was.

"We made a life," he said carefully, still watching her face. He could see she was taking this very seriously. Good. So was he.

She looked away, her eyes narrowing as she studied the horizon. "I'm horrified." She swallowed, her throat bobbing. "Petrified."

He didn't speak. He didn't trust himself to speak, not now, not with so much on the line.

Chantal closed her eyes, breathed deep. Folding her arms over her chest she tried to keep all the wild emotion inside. He had no idea what this meant. He had no idea how much was at stake. Her prenuptial with Armand had been very specific. There were certain duties, obligations, she'd agreed to. No affairs. No illicit conduct. No scandals.

Yes, she was widowed, but pregnant? Unmarried and pregnant? Talk about scandalous behavior. She could lose Lilly. She *would* lose Lilly. "I can't have this baby," she said, pressing her knuckled fists hard against her ribs. "I know it sounds cold, but it's the God's honest truth. The Thibaudets have been looking for a reason to get rid of me. An unplanned pregnancy would give them all the motive they need."

"You don't even like them."

"But my daughter inherits the throne. They could kick me out but keep her."

"That's not permissible by law."

"It is in La Croix. It's an old monarchy, not a democracy. The king and queen still wield incredible power."

"Including holding their own granddaughter hostage?"

Chantal shifted uncomfortably. "They don't see it that way."

His black eyebrows shot up. "You're defending them?"

"Of course not, but I have to be pragmatic."

Demetrius's expression turned brooding. His dark eyes narrowed fractionally, creases at the corners of his full mouth as he studied her taut features. "You're not even considering keeping the baby."

Her jaw ached from grinding her teeth so hard. She'd always wanted more children, she'd love another child, and deep within her she longed to hold one more baby, love one more baby, but she wasn't allowed to have more children.

The price of a pregnancy would be losing Lilly. Permanently.

"No," she answered huskily, breaking away from his piercing gaze. Drawing a shallow breath, she felt the pinch of her bra strap. Her breasts were already fuller. Her body heavier. She couldn't believe how quickly her body was changing, adjusting, growing.

Little baby. Her eyes stung and she bit the inside of her lip. She wanted the baby. She couldn't have the baby. It was horrendous. Heinous. No woman should ever have to be put in her position. To save one child, she couldn't have another.

"So that's it," he said, disgusted. "No discussion, no exploring other options—"

"What other options?" Her eyes blazed. "My daughter is the sole heir to the throne. She's already being groomed as the future queen. There's no way I can leave her in La Croix so I can come play house here!"

"Oh, that's all right, then. All the sacrifice, the loss of freedom, of choice, of love, of life…it's worth it as long as Lilly becomes queen?"

She flinched at his sarcasm. He didn't understand that for a royal there was no choice. For one born a Ducasse or a Thibaudet duty came first.

But Demetrius wasn't finished with her yet. "Are you sure, Princess, this isn't your ambition driving your daughter's future? Are you sure it isn't you that wants to be queen?"

Her head lifted in outrage and her eyes met his. "Being born royal is the last thing I'd wish upon a child, but Lilly is what Lilly is, just as I am what I am."

Her chest burned with bottled emotion. He'd hurt her, deeply. How could he suggest it was her own selfishness that kept Lilly trapped in La Croix? "And you know how much I love Lilly. You know I'd do anything for her, anything to secure her happiness."

"Including abort the child inside you."

CHAPTER ELEVEN

His words lanced deep. Her eyes filled with sudden tears, the shock and pain so deep. My God. How could he?

Staring at him, hurt, appalled, she felt her stomach curdle and heave. "You make me sick," she choked. Literally, she thought, stumbling to her feet. She rushed from her chair, back to her ensuite bathroom where she threw herself over the toilet as her stomach emptied again, and again.

Tears streamed from her eyes as she retched, the sourness in her mouth nothing compared to the fire in her heart. He didn't know. He couldn't know. She'd been through hell. She'd been slapped. Struck. Beaten. She'd endured the worst kind of humiliation to keep her daughter safe. Protected. The shame she'd endured had to be worth it. The bruises and tears couldn't be for nothing.

"I'm sorry." Demetrius's rough voice came from the doorway. "I was too blunt."

Clutching the rim of the toilet, the porcelain cool against her palms, she shook her head, tears still falling, the pain so hot and fresh that she couldn't master her emotions, that control seemed impossible. *Blunt? Was that all? How about harsh? Cruel?*

She stood, rinsed her face, patted it dry and walked out of the bathroom on trembling legs. She'd married Armand, was determined to love him, and he'd hurt her. Not just once. But repeatedly, over and over, and the abuse had lasted for years.

Exhausted, Chantal sat down on the foot of her bed. "I'd die if I lost her," she said hoarsely. The tears had stopped falling and yet she could still feel them on the inside. There was so much sadness there, so much pain buried in her heart, and if he thought she found any of this easy, then he didn't know her at all. Losing her parents, growing up fast to become the big sister Nic and Joelle needed, fighting to preserve the family name and interests...it'd been nothing but a battle for years. "She's all I have left. She's all I live for."

"But you have a new life to think of. And that life needs you, too."

"Oh, God." Chantal's voice broke, a mirror image of her heart, and she looked away, biting her lip so hard she tasted blood. In one hasty night she'd undone all that she'd worked so hard to do.

How could she have been so impulsive? So needy? So *desperate?*

"What's done is done." Demetrius sounded as controlled and as unemotional as she was distraught and broken. "The only thing to do now is move forward."

"I can't. Because I can't lose her. I won't. She's my heart."

He said nothing for a long moment and then she heard him sigh, a hard heavy sigh that seemed to come from deep within his soul.

She looked up, tucked a long strand of hair behind an ear. "I've talked to lawyers. The contract's water-tight."

"Do you have a copy?"

"At the châteaux. In my things."

"I'll request a copy. It wouldn't hurt for me to have a look at it, do some research." He moved into the bathroom, fetched the box of tissues from the marble counter and returned with it.

She took a tissue, wiped her eyes, blew her nose. "Won't do any good." She crumpled tissue in her hands, her chest aching so much it hurt to breathe. She didn't think she'd ever feel the same. To have another child—her cherished dream—but to lose Lilly? What kind of dream was that? "The contract is very specific."

"And it expressly forbids you from taking Lilly from La Croix?"

"The contract prevents me from moving, marrying, or having another child."

His narrowed gaze rested on her face. A small muscle pulled in his jaw. "I won't let them take her from you. We'll find a way to make this work."

"How?" She wiped fresh tears from her eyes and reached for yet another tissue.

"I don't know that yet, but I do know this—there are only two certainties in life—life and death. Everything else is negotiable."

He sounded so hard, so determined. But he didn't know the Thibaudets, didn't know the history. Armand had been there only child, the only son, and his death had changed them. Shut them down. Turned them into bitter, angry controlling people. They weren't going to lose Lilly. They had no one to replace her with. "They can't be bought."

"Maybe not with money."

"How else do you buy people?"

"There are lots of ways."

Her mouth, still so sour, dried. She swallowed convulsively. She needed to wash her face. Brush her teeth. Right now she felt like a mess. "How do you know all this?"

His lips curved but it was a ferocious expression, more snarl than smile. "You can thank my family for my extensive education. Due to their influence I understand what motivates them. People aren't that complicated, *pedhaki mou*. It's just a matter of handling a situation right."

"You're saying you think you could find a way to—" she broke off, searched for the word even as she searched his eyes "—pressure the Thibaudets into returning Lilly to me?"

"Pressure, manipulate, what's the difference?" He shrugged, the thick muscles in his shoulders and chest rippling beneath his loose linen shirt. "I don't really worry about the methods."

"You make it sound as if you were perhaps...not exactly on the right side of the law."

He stared down at her, the shadow of his beard making his jaw look wider, darker. "You understand correctly."

She recoiled and yet she wanted to know more. "How did Malik Nuri find you anyway?"

"We go back a long, long way and when Nuri explained your situation, the danger you're in, and I told him you needed someone good, someone tough, someone heartless. You needed to be protected at all cost.'' His lips curved in a small mocking smile. ''Nuri said that would be me.''

Even inside where the air was warm, Chantal felt chilled. ''You're far from heartless.''

''You don't know me.''

But they'd been together now nearly two weeks, and he'd proven to her that he was strong, focused, serious. He'd proven he wouldn't abandon her—he hadn't on the plane, and he didn't intend to now.

''You don't know me,'' he repeated even more quietly and her heart slowed. Her nerves in state of alert.

''Maybe I don't. But I trust you anyway.''

''You trust too easily then.''

''Why shouldn't I trust you?'' she demanded defiantly.

His dark eyes raked her, taking in her loose hair, her oval-shaped face, the simple dress that clung to her curves, revealing the soft swell of her breast, her smooth throat and bare shoulders, and all of her sweetness and vulnerability. ''Because I'm a man.''

''And?''

His expression turned mocking. ''I'm territorial. Unforgiving. And I protect that which is mine.''

Her veins were dancing now, adrenaline shooting through her. ''I didn't know I'd become yours.''

''You're here.''

''*You* brought me here.''

''Exactly.''

She tensed, growing angry all over again. She didn't understand why he should make her feel this way...so frustrated...so filled with wild and conflicting emotions. There was no reason to feel conflicting emotion. She should want off his island. She should want away from him. She should want nothing to do with him.

''And then there is the baby, which is mine,'' he said, still watching her intently. Possessively. ''It's my duty to protect both of you now.''

''No. It's your *duty* to get me home. Back to Lilly. That was the deal. That was the promise you made me.''

''Before I knew about my child.''

His child. What about *her* child? What about Lilly, her daughter she hadn't seen in three weeks now. "There is no baby yet. I'm barely a week late. My period could still come—"

"It won't."

Her heart pounded. She felt sick all over again. "I haven't spent the last nine years denying myself everything I need, to make a stupid mistake now. And you can't pretend you don't know that I've sacrificed everything—including my pride and dignity—so Lilly can be happy."

"Stop hiding behind your daughter."

"I'm not. I'm protecting her. And if you can't see the difference then I don't know what I ever saw in you!"

"I see the difference. And you know damn well what you saw in me." His gaze locked with hers. "But this isn't the time to fight that one. We've enough to cope with at the moment."

At least he was being calm. Relatively reasonable. She appreciated that someone could keep a level head right now.

"There's no reason to panic," he added. "We've time. You won't show for months. That will buy us a lot of time. And later, if need be, you can dress to hide the pregnancy. Everything seems overwhelming today, but that's part shock, part hormones. Trust me, we can make this work. We can have this baby."

It wasn't until after he left, and she'd begun changing into her swimsuit, that his words hit her forcibly. *We can have this baby.*

Hands going numb, she struggled to slide the slender strap of her black tank style suit over her shoulder. What exactly did he mean?

Brow creasing, she straightened the strap on her and adjusted the suit along her hipbones. When he said 'we', what was he suggesting? Intending?

He knew she couldn't retire from public life and play house. He knew she'd never become Mrs. Demetrius Mantheakis. How did he propose they *have* this baby?

Wrapping the black and white silk sarong around her hips, Chantal tugged a straw hat low on her head and went to the pool. One of the housemaids brought her a light meal and after eating the toasted ham sandwich, she settled into a lounge chair and tried to lose herself in a book.

But she couldn't read, and even the magazines that Demetrius had bought for her were unable to hold her interest. Her thoughts were scattered.

The warm afternoon breeze brushed her skin, and closing her eyes she could picture the baby inside her, could actually feel the baby in her arms now.

She could feel the small weight of warmth against her chest, feel the sweetness, the softness, the tender way babies curved against the breast, their little backs, their little bodies, their hands nestled to their mouths.

The thick emotion inside her grew, swelling, a press against her heart, against her throat. She swallowed, pin pricks of pain against her eyes.

She'd never been able to savor Lilly's pregnancy. From the moment she conceived Lilly, Armand had been angry. Bitter. He hadn't liked Chantal slim, and he hadn't liked her pregnant. Nothing she did was right. Nothing she did was okay. And as she grew, bigger, bigger, Armand's temper flared. After she gave birth, Armand's disgust seemed to know no bound.

He hated her. That was the only conclusion she could come up with. And yet she didn't know what she'd done to provoke such virulent contempt. She'd done everything she was supposed to do. Married him. Slept with him. Conceived his child. What had she denied him? Nothing.

Maybe that's why he hated her.

She'd been his doormat. She was nothing to him but a place for him to wipe his feet as he came and went. Hello, slam. Good-bye, slam.

The lump in her throat threatened to choke her. It hurt to breathe. It hurt to feel, to remember.

Lilly's first year had been a blur of tears and pain. She could remember the slaps, the fists, the punches only because she remembered trying to hold back the tears, stifling the cries, because she didn't want Lilly to hear. She didn't want her shriek to wake the baby.

Don't wake the baby.

Chantal closed her eyes, tightly. It wasn't fair. It had never been fair, but what could she do? Where could she go? With

Lilly's birth she'd effectively given up her freedom, given up her name, her voice, her country. And if she wanted out, she could leave, but leave without Lilly. And God knew, God and all his angels and his eyes and ears knew, there was no way she'd leave Lilly.

Not then. Not now. Not ever.

She reached up, swiped a tear from her lower lashes. Swiped another, chest aching, heartbroken. Wouldn't it be amazing to have a baby, and be free to love the baby? Wouldn't it be incredible to have this baby and just hold the baby, hour after hour, night after night?

She could see herself lying on her side in bed, see her arm wrapped protectively around her swaddled infant and the baby would smell of powder and lotion and love.

"You can't cry." The lounge chair shifted as Demetrius sat down next to her. He tilted her chin up, shook his head. "Crying isn't the answer."

She couldn't whisk the tears away fast enough. "I'm sorry. I can't seem to stop." She scrubbed at her eyes, her throat so raw, her eyes burning like mad. She wanted to pluck them out. Wanted to tear her heart out. She couldn't stand so much emotion. So many memories. So much buried pain. She'd never really dealt with the memories before, the reality of what had happened in her marriage with Armand. She'd thought the best way to recover was to ignore the facts. If she didn't think about it, the truth would fade, the painful details would go away. If she didn't let herself dwell on bad things, the bad things wouldn't hurt her anymore.

But the bad things had hurt her anyway. The bad things had hurt…bad.

"I should be cried out," she said, struggling to get her voice normal, wanting to find calm again. She was exhausted, truly exhausted. She honestly didn't think she could handle much more of this.

"It's the hormones."

"I didn't feel this teary with Lilly—" She broke off, bit her cheek, her eyes lifting, meeting his. That wasn't true, she thought, sick. She might have felt this way with Lilly. She didn't remember. She didn't remember anything about her pregnancy with Lilly except for a pervasive fear. Don't hit me. Don't hit me. It could hurt the baby. Please God, if he hits me, let him hit my face, not my body, never my body.

She placed a cold hand to her face, fingers covering her cheek, her mouth. She was going to be sick again if she wasn't careful.

"I won't have anymore of this." Demetrius voice, hard, tough, unyielding, cut through the fog of her misery. "The crying will only make you sick. It's time for dinner. Go bathe, dress, meet me in half an hour, yes? I won't have you late, and I won't have any more sad faces tonight. Understand?"

She nodded, a wobbily nod, but she got to her feet and drew her sarong snugger around her hips and left the pool for her room. He watched her go and then he, too, headed to his room to shower and dress for dinner.

In the shower, Demetrius turned the water on full force and let the hard spray rain down on him, but the drumming pulse of water did little to ease the tension pounding in his head.

It was easy to protect Chantal here, on the Rock. The families living on the island ensured the safety of the island's perimeter, and the villa itself boasted top of the line security technology— alarmed windows and doors, motion detectors, glass protectors, hidden cameras. He'd know if anyone entered the house. He'd know if anyone left the house. He'd know if anyone called at the house. It was his house. His safe haven. He knew if Chantal remained here, she and the baby would be protected. But she wouldn't be here indefinitely, and he feared what would happen once she returned to her real world.

Toweling off, his whole body still felt hot, hard, his temper simmering just below the surface. Nothing better happen to the princess or the baby. No one better touch them. No man better dare.

He didn't trust himself—didn't trust the outcome—if anyone threatened her now.

He'd always been protective of women, but pregnant women? It was a state of grace, a plane of light and beauty. If he still had faith, his faith was in life, the ability to resurrect in the face of suffering and death.

He, who thought he'd lost everything, had a chance to be a father again, he had a chance to hold his child in his arms, love a child. He saw hope where there had been none.

The key was keeping them here where he and his people could watch over her, ensure that no one would get too close, defend her in the event that security broke down.

But security wouldn't break down, he reminded himself, lathering his face and neck, preparing to shave. Security was his specialty. Security was what he knew. He owned the best equipment. Employed the smartest people. Put his staff through the hardest tests and drills.

His people wouldn't let him down.

Rinsing off his razor with hot water, he reached up for one last stroke on the side of his neck and somehow he caught the skin at an angle and blood spurted through the shaving foam.

Demetrius stared at his reflection in the mirror, stared at the stream of bright blood, and his body went cold. Ice cold.

Katina.

He dropped the razor into the basin and stepped back, grabbed a hand towel and blotted his neck, wiping the remainder of the shaving cream away.

He hadn't protected her.

Tears of rage burned the back of his eyes but the tears didn't come. The tears wouldn't come. He tossed the hand towel onto the counter and stalked from the bathroom to his bedroom and dressed. He'd failed Katina but he wasn't going to fail Chantal. Chantal might not want him, might not love him, but he wouldn't leave her side.

He had a job to do. And he'd damn well do it.

Descending the staircase, Demetrius spotted Chantal wandering outside on the terrace. She was wearing a simple blush colored gown, thin straps, smooth delicate bodice, and a long straight skirt falling to her ankles. She'd drawn her hair back in a loose ponytail low at her nape, leaving her neck and shoulders bare.

On the candle lit terrace she looked fragile. Vulnerable. Nothing like the remote princess photographed in glossy international magazines. Nothing like the sophisticated beauty lauded for her exquisite fashion sense.

Here, with the moon rising overhead and the sea breeze lifting tendrils of her dark hair, he could believe she'd been badly used by her late husband. Without the fashionably cut coats and suits, fitted skirts and slacks, without the Italian leather heels and the chic designer purses, hats, expertly coiffed hair the woman—the real woman—was endearingly simple. Sweet. Touching.

She'd never had a normal life. From birth to her marriage, to her husband's death, she'd been indoctrinated, disciplined, dictated to.

She'd belonged to everyone but herself.

And now he was wanting to do what all the others had done: take control of her life, seize power while he could, wrestle the decision making process from her.

He was no different from the others, was he?

Drawing a heavy breath, he stood there, considering her, considering their options. If he let her go today she'd end up seriously hurt—or worse. If he let her return to La Croix with another bodyguard she might choose to end the pregnancy. If he kept her here, she'd be safe, and she'd give him the child he wanted more than he'd wanted anything since...since...ever.

He swallowed. He was no virtuous man.

Abruptly Chantal turned, spotted him in the doorway. "How long have you been standing there?" she asked.

"Not long."

She didn't know if she should believe him. Didn't know what to believe at all anymore. Funny how just a glimpse of him and she felt lost, drowning beneath waves of contradictory emotion.

Her first reaction when she spotted him had been pleasure—there he was—the man who made her feel like a real woman again. And immediately following that initial response, was a second one—anger. How dare he try to dictate to her? How dare he try to use the pregnancy to control her? She'd had enough of men dominating her, speaking down to her, trying to plan her life for her.

A maid appeared, bobbed her head, murmured something to Demetrius. Chantal watched as he immediately left the terrace, returning to the house. He wasn't gone long, and when he came back five minutes later, he was carrying a sheet of paper.

Wordlessly Demetrius handed it to her.

It was a faxed letter, a letter initially printed on Melio palace stationery. The letter had been written by the palace secretary. *Princess Chantal, we regret to inform you...*

Her hand trembled. She looked up, swallowed, shook her head. Couldn't be. Impossible. She'd had to have read the telegram wrong.

Blinking, Chantal forced away tears, and read the message again.

We regret to inform you of the death of Her Royal Highness...

It was the same.

Ice swallowed her, engulfing her, freezing everything from her heart to her trembling hand. "Demetrius," she whispered his name, her voice failing her. "She's gone."

"I'm sorry."

She swayed a little, stared at the words blurring beneath her vision. *We regret to inform you...we regret...we...we...*

She felt his hand at her waist, felt him guide her to a chair. She allowed herself to be seated, swallowing around the sourness filling her mouth. "Grandmama's gone."

"When are the services?"

"Soon." She clenched her fist, wrinkling the fax. "I can't believe—" She broke off, struggled to take a breath. "I knew it could happen, but...you never do think...you never want to think..."

His hand lightly rubbed her back, calming, soothing. "I'll make arrangements for us to leave first thing in the morning."

She was downstairs early, her things packed by one of the house maids in a leather suitcase, formal dresses zippered into a matching garment bag, make up and hair appliances in another. Somehow she'd arrived on the island with nothing and yet she was leaving now like the princess she was.

Chantal had dressed this morning in a rather severe dark navy suit, the only ornamentation the gold military style buttons on the jacket. She'd twisted her hair up into her traditional chignon, the style she wore most often for public appearances. She couldn't believe this appearance was for her grandmother's funeral. How many funerals had she attended now? Her parents. Her husband's. Now Grandmama's.

Demetrius sat at the back of the plane, left Chantal alone with her own thoughts. They flew into Melio's private airport, the terminal reserved for the royal family and visiting dignitaries. On arriving they discovered the Thibaudets had just flown in from La Croix and Chantal could barely sit still in the back of the limo on the way to the palace.

It was horrible, horrible returning like this, but at least she'd see Lilly.

But on reaching the palace and being ushered into the Thibaudets guest suite, Chantal discovered they hadn't brought Lilly with them after all. Chantal swayed on her feet, stunned. She'd waited so long to see her daughter. She'd counted on having Lilly's company, counted on finally being a family again.

Again Demetrius remained in the background, shadowing Chantal but refraining from speaking. Chantal was aware of his presence but couldn't turn to him, afraid that if she looked at him, or spoke to him, her fragile control would break. She'd wanted Lilly so badly. She'd missed Lilly so much. Three and a half weeks without her daughter. It was a lifetime.

Not even Joelle or Nic could comfort Chantal that afternoon. Nauseous, exhausted, she lay on her bed until the evening reception where the Ducasse royals were to receive visiting dignitaries. She managed to greet guests for two hours until she couldn't smile another gracious smile or speak another grateful word. In the back of her mind she felt only rage and pain.

She'd done everything ever asked of her. How could the Thibaudets keep Lilly from her now?

Finally she left the grand salon and escaped to her room. Demetrius climbed the stairs behind her. She felt him so strongly that her whole body tingled with heat and need.

At her bedroom door she faced him. She knew he'd remain outside her door, ever vigilant. But she didn't want him outside her room. She wanted him in it. And she didn't want him for sex, but for his warmth and strength. "I need you," she whispered.

"I'll be out here—"

"You know that's not what I mean."

His dark eyes met hers. They burned tonight, burned with a silent fire. "I can't do my job here, and the job you want in there."

She flushed at the tone of his voice. *The job in there.* He was reminding her most ungently that he believed all she wanted him for was sex. Her eyes burned, she struggled to smile. "Was it such a job to sleep with me?"

"No. You have a gorgeous body. A very sweet and sexy body, and a lot of men would be happy to give you what you want. But if I have to pick between satisfying your need, Princess, and protecting your life, I'll stay outside the bedroom."

CHAPTER TWELVE

CHANTAL murmured a strangled good night and shut the door, but once inside her room, she crawled into bed fully dressed.

She didn't have Lilly. She didn't have Demetrius. And he was wrong. It wasn't sex she wanted. She wanted him. *Him.* She wanted his arms, and his chest, and his heart beating beneath her ear. But she was afraid of what he'd do—afraid of what he'd do to her life—if he knew how she much she cared for him, how much she wanted the happy ever after ending with him.

Chantal was sick twice before breakfast, and then there was the stiff, silent motorcade ride to the cathedral for the services. Chantal knew her sisters were watching her but she couldn't bring herself to speak. She felt miserable. Absolutely ill-sick to her stomach, sick at heart.

During the memorial service, Chantal had to escape not once, but twice, to throw up in the ladies' restroom.

Hunched over the toilet, she heard footsteps enter the bathroom, a small squeak of the door. They clicked across the floor, the sound definitively female. Chantal spied high heels. "Princess Chantal?" the female voice asked, concerned.

"Everything's fine," Chantal answered as the door to the stall pushed open. From the corner of her eye she saw a woman peer in and then another wave of nausea hit and Chantal was hugging the toilet hard.

The door squeaked, open, shut. The woman was gone.

A moment later, the door opened again. "Chantal?" It was Demetrius's voice this time. "Who was that?"

"I don't know." And then she was getting sick again, and her sour churning stomach fueled fresh panic. What was she going to do? Oh God, how long could she hide this from her family...from the world?

"I'm just outside," he said.

"I know."

The rest of the funeral passed in a blur. Between the morning sickness, and the sorrow over her grandmother's passing, Chantal could barely focus on the external events. Dimly she knew that the ceremony itself was beautiful, the music soaring high between the elegant columns, floating up to the cream and gold ceiling. It was a beautiful day, and radiant sunlight poured through the stained-glass windows. It was the kind of day Grandmama would have loved. She'd relished her life on Melio, embracing the sunshine and the long growing season. Grandmama had loved her roses, the rare coral hued and white camellias, the dogwood tree she'd imported and coaxed into blooming a vivid pink every spring.

But the service ended, the last song was sung, the casket removed, and later, after the cathedral emptied, the last condolences were accepted, the last hand shaken.

The graveside internment was private, and this, too, took everything from Chantal. She stood with her grandfather and sisters in the beautiful family cemetery, trying to keep from thinking about the gravestones just behind her, the two beautiful marble stones with her mother and father's names on them.

This wasn't the time to remember. This wasn't the time to think about anything other than Grandfather who looked as if he'd just had the life beat out of him.

Holding back tears, she moved closer to Grandpapa and slipped her hand into his. His hand shook, his skin thin, delicate like crepe. How he'd aged since Grandmama took sick. He'd lost the fire that made him King Remi, fading instead to a shadow of whom he'd once been.

Prayers were said, a murmur of voices around them, and then the casket began its slow descent.

Grandfather's fingers tightened painfully around hers.

She squeezed his fingers back, trying to let him know she was there. But it was a dreadful loss. He and Grandmama had been together nearly sixty-five years. Sixty-five years sharing a room, a bed, a life with someone. How did one say goodbye? How did one ever let go?

Chantal looked up, spotted Demetrius standing on the opposite side of the grave, his narrowed gaze scanning the surrounding grounds. Then he turned his head and looked at her. She had no idea what he was thinking from his expression, there was no tenderness in the hard set of his eyes and jaw. What did he feel about her?

It had been a long twenty-four hours, Demetrius thought, keeping vigil across from Chantal. He couldn't wait until the services ended so he could get Chantal back to the palace, back to a semblance of safety. She was so exposed at the services, both at the cathedral and here, and he felt her vulnerability acutely. It was impossible to get close enough to her today, not with her family taking precedence, but he also couldn't shake the feeling that they were being watched. That *she* was being watched.

Demetrius couldn't explain how he knew, but he just felt the prickle of danger, that uneasy sense that things were not right. Even with additional detectives on the job, and heightened security from Demetrius's Paris and Athens offices, no one had successfully pinpointed the threat yet. Right now anyone from La Croix could be the suspect. Anyone could be targeting her.

It was a quiet ride back to the palace. Demetrius rode in the second limousine with Chantal and her youngest sister, Joelle. He saw the younger princess glance at him, curious, worried. She had Chantal's coloring, but was taller, quite slender, and her blue eyes had more green in them—making them almost turquoise.

Seeing Princess Joelle's wide anxious gaze as she glanced from her sister to him, made him realize how innocent—how *sheltered*—Chantal must have been when she married Armand. She'd known nothing about the world at large. She couldn't have even imagined the abuse she'd suffer at her new husband's hands.

They were silent as they ascended the broad circular palace staircase. A quiet family dinner had been planned for later in the evening and Demetrius would see Chantal to her room, and wait while she changed for the meal. But she'd only been inside her room for a moment when she reappeared, and when she opened the door her face was pale.

"Demetrius," she choked out his name, opened her door wider to permit him in.

In her room, a dozen long stemmed roses lay on her exposed

pillowcase, wrapped in gold tissue and tied with a black bow. The roses were dead.

"Have you touched them?" he asked, immediately holding her back.

She shook her head. "No. But there's a card."

"I'm interested in the card, but I want fingerprints first."

Chantal exhaled slowly, rubbed her arms, chilled despite her somber black suit. "This isn't a very nice secret admirer."

"No." He wrapped an arm around her waist and drew her against him. "And the fact that he can access your bedroom, within your family's home, worries me."

All she could think about was going home, seeing Lilly. "Me, too." She drew a shaky breath. "I wish I was in La Croix. Couldn't we go tonight?"

He pulled her closer. "It's too late to fly tonight. I need to arrange security, as well as submit a flight plan, but I promise we'll leave first thing in the morning."

She nodded, shivered. "So where do I sleep?"

"In my hotel suite, with me."

His hotel was luxurious, his suite on the top floor. Chantal noticed the security detail parked out front of the hotel, as well as the men stationed outside Demetrius's suite.

Unlocking the door to his rooms, Demetrius did a quick search, checking closets, bathrooms, beneath the massive king-size bed. "Not taking any chances," he said, catching her eye.

"You never do."

His lips curved, a shadow of a smile. "Not with you." He peeled off his coat, removed the leather holster strap he wore beneath his arm. "Hungry?"

He'd been armed. She shouldn't have been surprised, of course he'd be armed when she was the target of some madman, but glancing at the gun sitting on top of the marble bar counter, she shivered. She hated weapons, had never approved of guns. "I wouldn't mind something light," she said, wanting to get something inside her stomach before the morning sickness returned.

"I'll order," he said, reaching for the phone, "Why don't you relax in the tub?"

The bathtub was enormous, and Chantal poured the rich herbal bath gel provided by the hotel beneath the running tap, filling the steamy bathroom with the heady scent of lavender and citrus.

Eyes closed, and chin deep in warm, fragrant water Chantal heard the knock on the bathroom door, and opened her eyes. "Dinner here?"

"No, not for another five or ten minutes." The door opened and Demetrius leaned against the doorway, eyes hooded, expression pensive. "The detectives have finished dusting for fingerprints at the palace, and they intend to run the fingerprints with local databases, but it could take awhile."

She felt Demetrius's frustration. He didn't like that the investigation was moving so slowly. He was a results man. He backed up his talk with action. "They're doing they're best, right?"

He shook his head wearily. "I wish I had you back on the Rock. I felt better with you there, I could sleep."

She felt a pang. "You're not sleeping?"

"I worry about you being so vulnerable. Being pregnant I—" He broke off, looked away, gaze narrowing. He drew a deep breath, and then another, and yet there was a hint of desperation beneath the surface, an intense emotion that rendered him vulnerable.

He was struggling, truly struggling and Chantal sat up in the bath, her heart wrenched. "Demetrius, I'm pregnant, not sick."

"Yes, but if someone got close to you, someone had access to you—" Again he bit back the words and yet Chantal understood what he was trying to say.

He was afraid she couldn't defend herself properly, afraid that in her condition she'd be even more helpless than before. "Come here," she said softly, extending a hand to him. "Don't stand so far away."

He hesitated before approaching the tub, and dropping to her side.

With him crouched beside the bath, they were eye level and his expression looked tortured. He wasn't the iron man tonight, far from invincible, and Chantal thought she'd never cared so much for him. Gently she reached out to touch his face, his dark jaw bristly. "I don't want you to worry." She tried to smile but her heart felt full and far too tender. "You're doing everything humanly possible to keep me safe and I have full confidence in you, and your security detail.''

''Mistakes happen,'' he said bitterly.

''We can't help that.''

''But they shouldn't happen.''

She caressed his prominent cheekbone. He was a man that would never shirk his duty. He'd never abandon those weaker, or those in need. ''We're human.'' For the past years she hadn't liked herself, seeing only her weaknesses, feeling only her helplessness, and yet suddenly she felt calm, she felt settled. Demetrius brought balance to her life. Perspective. ''And if you honestly believe I only wanted you for sex than you're a bigger fool than—''

He cut her words off with a kiss. Chantal felt the smoldering heat of it all the way through and her lips parted beneath his.

Minutes later when he finally lifted his head, he strummed her soft lips with his thumb. ''I'm no fool, Chantal. I know there's a lot more here than sex.'' At this his dark eyes glimmered with a hidden smile. ''But being wanted for my body is kind of a turn on.''

He left her to finish her bath but later after room service had delivered dinner and Chantal was sitting in the hotel robe at the dining table with Demetrius, he returned to the subject of the investigation. What the detectives had discovered, and hadn't yet discovered, had been weighing on him all evening. The last thing he wanted to do was upset her on top of such a long, disturbing day, but he needed her help.

''They've had a look at the card left with the flowers in your room at the palace,'' he said.

Chantal looked up at him, her soup spoon suspended midair. ''And?''

He wasn't going to tell her the exact message on the card, it was far too sinister and the peculiar wording had sent chills through him. The stalker had implied he'd be waiting for her in La Croix, that he knew she'd be heading there next and he'd be the first to welcome her home. And the way the word *welcome* had been written in a suspicious reddish ink that wasn't ink at all but dried blood, made Demetrius's skin crawl.

"The card was signed 'S'," Demetrius said evenly, hiding the depth of his concern. Momentum was building. The situation had become extreme. "Do you know anyone by 'S', first name? Last name? Anyone from La Croix come to mind?"

She leaned forward, propped her elbows on the table, and chewed her thumb. Her forehead furrowed as she seemed to be mentally cataloging names, faces, but after a minute she shook her head. "Any number of names start with an 'S.' Sabina, Sabrina, Suzette, but no one that I personally know."

"How about men?"

"I can't think of anyone."

"Simon? Silvio?"

Again she shook her head. "I'm sorry. Doesn't ring a bell."

"That's all right. The detectives are still running tests, trying to match the fingerprint." But inwardly he sighed. He was tired. His brain barely functioned these past few days. He knew he needed more sleep than what he was getting but he didn't trust anyone else to watch her, was afraid of what would happen if he fell asleep.

Later when Chantal yawned, he suggested she turn in, get some rest before the flight home. "You're going to need your energy," he gently teased. "Your daughter is going to be thrilled to see you."

Chantal immediately brightened. "I can't wait. It's been forever since I saw her." And then she hesitated, her expression uncertain. "Are you going to sleep in here with me?" She swallowed, color suffusing her cheeks. "I'd like you, to. It might be our last—" She broke off, bit her lip. "Things will be different in La Croix."

"I know." Very different, he silently added, looking at her for a long, excruciating moment, knowing he had no idea what she'd do once back in La Croix, knowing he had no right to ask her to sacrifice Lilly's happiness for his child's life. But he wanted the baby. He wanted Chantal and the baby desperately.

"I'll come in a little later," he said, squashing his emotion, refusing to let her see how much he hated escorting her back into the face of danger. Every instinct in him insisted he take her away from La Croix back to the Rock. His driving need was to protect her and the baby, not deliver her like a sacrificial lamb to the Thibaudet châteaux. "I've some calls to make, and I haven't finished finalizing our security detail for the morning."

He kissed her at the door of the bedroom, kissed her knowing this might very well be the last time he held her like this, and then he clamped control over his emotion and need, and broke away. "Get some sleep."

He turned to leave but her voice stopped. "Demetrius, if Lilly were your daughter, what would you do?"

For a long moment he couldn't answer, then he sighed heavily. There was no way he could lie to her. "I'd do what you're doing. I'd protect Lilly and her future with every bone in my body."

In the bedroom Chantal curled on her side in the big downy bed, staring at the bedroom door which he'd left open a crack. She could see him from the bed. He'd finished his calls, he'd shut down his computer, and now he stood in the semidarkness of the living room, facing the marble fireplace. His shirt was unbuttoned, leaving his chest naked.

He was deep in thought, his hard features severe, and yet she'd never seen him look more beautiful.

He was so troubled. He was agonizing over the baby. She didn't blame him. She was tormented, too.

If there was a way to do this—have the baby, be with Demetrius, keep Lilly—she'd jump at the chance, but at the moment she didn't see a way out. Couldn't see how she'd ever escape the repressive Thibaudets.

Demetrius hoped Chantal was finally asleep. He'd heard her tossing and turning in the bedroom earlier but in the last half hour the room had grown quiet.

He should try to get some sleep, too, but he couldn't go in there, couldn't climb into that bed and be near her and feel her warmth and softness and then climb out in the morning knowing he'd never hold her again, knowing he'd never be so close.

He raised his hands, leaned against the mantle, feeling the muscles in his back harden.

He was in over his head. His stomach knotted. For the first time in his career, he'd lost perspective. He wasn't doing his job anymore. Instead of thinking about the princess's safety, he was obsessing about his own needs.

It shouldn't matter that Chantal didn't want what he wanted. It shouldn't change the way he did his job, and yet he knew he'd lost focus. Knew he was distracted by thoughts of the baby, concerns about the future. A good bodyguard needed a clear cool head. Demetrius had lost his.

He'd been kidding himself when he said he was the best man for the job. It'd been selfish on his part. He hadn't wanted to leave her, hadn't wanted to let go of her. But it was time he faced the truth. His personal interest was jeopardizing her welfare. The fact was, he cared too much for her, and he cared deeply, passionately, about the baby. Unfortunately his needs, his desires, were influencing his thinking.

Earlier tonight he'd put in a call to his office, requested the services of two of his best men. They were both excellent bodyguards, and he trusted them implicitly. It was time they stepped in and did the job he couldn't do anymore.

He gripped the edge of the mantel, muscles in his arms and shoulders tensing all over again.

He'd discovered things that could free Chantal, but it had come at such a price for Lilly that he couldn't tell her. Prince Armand Thibaudet had lived a secret life. Prince Armand wasn't the obedient son his family pretended he'd been.

The Thibaudets had married their son to Chantal to clean up his image. As the eldest of the Ducasse princesses, she was widely loved and admired. Although she was young at the time the engagement was announced, she was also smart, elegant, educated. Chantal was to bring class to a classless son of a bitch, Demetrius concluded bitterly.

She'd been used, and she'd been wronged.

But as Chantal had said, it wasn't about her anymore, it was about Lilly, and if Demetrius revealed what he knew, he'd get what he wanted—Chantal and the baby—but it'd destroy what Chantal wanted for Lilly. It'd destroy Lilly's happiness, her security, her future.

The child had already lost her father. Demetrius didn't believe he had the right to strip her of her title, take her from her home.

He loved Chantal so much that he loved what she loved, and she loved Lilly. Dearly. Deeply. It was one of the things he loved about her most—that she was such a devoted mother, that she'd put her daughter first, time and again.

Exhausted, Demetrius released the mantle. He'd started his business to protect others from suffering. He'd used his own pain to ensure that others wouldn't hurt as he did, and that's what he'd do now. He'd protect Chantal and Lilly. No matter the cost.

CHAPTER THIRTEEN

MORNING arrived, as did breakfast and a stack of international newspapers. Demetrius woke Chantal with a pot of tea and toast. "Plain toast," he said, setting the plate on the nightstand next to her. "We'll leave as soon as you've eaten."

She struggled to sit up, momentarily confused by her whereabouts. Then her grogginess vanished as she realized what he'd just said. They'd be on their way to La Croix soon. She'd be with Lilly before noon.

"I'm also bringing in two new bodyguards," he added tersely. "They're men I've known for years. Alexi will be on the flight. Louis will be at the châteaux. They've been briefed. They know everything I know."

She stared at him for a long moment. His voice was already detached, his body language reserved. "Where are you going?"

"I'll be around. Just not in the foreground."

He was letting her go, she thought, fighting panic, he was already stepping away. "I don't want anyone else."

He struggled to smile, and on him it looked almost frightening. "I'm still traveling with you today. I wouldn't leave you now. I've no intention of leaving you until you're safe."

Her eyes stung. She felt the distance yawning between them. "And when I'm safe?"

He shrugged. "That's for you to decide."

She blinked, but tears were filling her eyes. "I don't want to say goodbye."

"When this is all over, you'll know how to find me. I'll give you my number—"

"Okay. Great." She couldn't do this now, couldn't start the day like this. What did he mean? What about their baby? "I think I'll just get dressed."

The flight was short, from take off to landing, lasting barely forty-five minutes. On board the jet, Chantal was just about to

153

ask Demetrius for one of the newspapers she'd seen him fold and stash in his briefcase, when the plane began to descend.

The plane hit a pocket of turbulence and bounced and she was suddenly vividly reminded of the day they'd met, that terrifying plunge to the earth. Demetrius also seemed to remember, and he looked up, and smiled at her, the first real smile she'd seen in days.

"Frightened?"

Only of being without him, she thought. "No."

They touched ground without a problem, the landing so smooth it felt like they'd touched down on glass. The jet parked in front of the terminal, and Demetrius let the new bodyguard, Alexi, disembark first, then he and Chantal filed off, stepping out into the bright morning light. It was a beautiful day. Clear, sunny, not a cloud in the sky.

They walked swiftly across the tarmac and entered the cool dim terminal. It wouldn't be a long drive to the châteaux. A half hour at most and Demetrius had a car and driver waiting.

Alexi was moving toward the exit. The pilot had promised to carry the luggage to the car. Everything was running smoothly, Demetrius thought. Too smoothly, a little voice mocked inside his head.

He frowned. And yet instinctively he slowed his pace, realizing that Chantal had stopped walking. Glancing down, he saw a ribbon of worry between her fine dark brows. She was looking at something beyond the terminal window, and she was puzzled.

Demetrius tried to see what had caught her attention. The limo. The driver. Alexi at the terminal door.

His narrowed gaze scanned the nearly empty terminal, noted the young attendant at the desk and he shook his head, feeling stupid.

Something was wrong. But what?

His skin fairly crawled as they continued walking toward the door. Every cell in his body was alert as his sixth sense told him to be careful. But careful of what, and more importantly *where?*

Stepping closer to Chantal, he tried to tell himself that nothing was going to happen, that he was here and Alexi was here and they were nearly at the car.

But then the sliding glass doors opened. Demetrius felt a chill. The limousine driver had left the curb outside and entered the building.

Wrong.

A driver never left his car.

Yet right now the driver was heading their way and Demetrius went cold. The driver was nondescript, a middle aged man with fair, thinning hair, but it wasn't his physical appearance which struck Demetrius as wrong. It was the way he was looking at Chantal. His eyes looked hollow, vacant...and he was staring at the princess. And only the princess.

The driver was the danger.

"Do you know him?" Demetrius demanded harshly, drawing closer to her, wishing Alexi was closer, wanting to shield Chantal completely but knowing it was impossible now. She was exposed. He'd left her exposed.

"Yes." Her voice sounded faint. Scared.

Her fear reinforced his worry, and Demetrius felt the muscles in his neck thicken, tighten, tension building through his chest, torso, legs. "Where do you know him from?"

Chantal touched his arm, fingers squeezing his forearm muscle. "Stefano worked for Armand. He was once his driver, and now drives Phillipe and Catherine."

"That's his name?" he managed calmly, grateful to be so cold, so clearheaded. His mouth tasted faintly metallic. *Stefano. S.*

S. The infamous S that had haunted them these past few weeks.

Without taking his eyes off Stefano, Demetrius slid a possessive arm around Chantal's waist. "He's not the driver I requested."

She leaned against him, slipping her body even closer to his, tucking her shoulder beneath his arm. "I should have thought of him before. He's always been a bit odd around me. He doesn't drive me anymore. We had a problem awhile back—"

"We need to get you out of here," He interrupted roughly, not sure where to take her, only knowing that he would not let Chantal be hurt.

He needed Alexi. He needed the backup immediately.

Demetrius called out to Alexi in Greek, alerting him to the danger, and before Alexi could move, Demetrius saw Stefano reach inside his coat.

Stefano moved fast.

Demetrius had just a split-second to register the flash of shiny silver. A gun. Stefano was armed. He'd drawn a gun.

Adrenaline kicked in and everything seemed to happen at once.

Stepping in front of Chantal, he ordered her down even as he pulled his own weapon.

Chantal felt frozen in place. "Get down!" Demetrius's hoarse command echoed in her ears and for a moment she didn't understand, and then it all became crystal clear. Stefano had a gun.

Demetrius had drawn his gun.

She threw herself at the ground as a loud pop reverberated through the terminal. There was another pop and she saw Stefano stagger, and fall.

Demetrius had shot him.

She was up again, on her feet, even as Demetrius rushed to Stefano's side to disarm him. Stefano was on the ground but he was swearing horrendous curses, shouting venomous things at Chantal, hateful names that made her want to throw up, and then Alexi was there, putting his body between her and the others. "You need to go to the car," the young Greek bodyguard said.

She shook her head. "I have to stay with Demetrius."

"He wants you to go."

"No." She pushed against Alexi, but her arms were weak, her body was trembling all over. Hot, cold, terror and shock washed over her in waves.

The wail of sirens pierced the air and moments later a stream of blue and white police cars streaked across the parking lot, drawing up at random angles before the terminal entrance.

The police descended, flooding the building, roughly pulling Demetrius to his feet while Stefano remained on the ground.

Chantal struggled against Alexi as Demetrius was handcuffed. What were they handcuffing him for? "Let me go," she begged, watching the police push Demetrius out the door, toward a waiting police car.

Alexi at least allowed her to the door and standing at the glass, her eyes met Demetrius's as he was shoved into the back of the car. He looked calm, she thought, defiant.

Turning she saw Stefano lifted and strapped onto a gurney before he was wheeled from the building. Then the police car and ambulance streaked off, sirens shrieking.

"That's the end of that," Alexi said, escorting her outside. The limousine was still there but now there was no driver.

Alexi made a phone call. Ten minutes later a black sedan pulled up in front of the terminal. "We'll take you to the châteaux," Alexi said as they entered the car.

"I'd rather go to the police station."

"There's nothing you can do right now."

"I have to go anyway."

Alexi shook his head. He was a younger version of Demetrius. Fierce. Unsmiling. But he acquiesced. "Then we'll go."

The drive to the police station was long, and Chantal stared blindly out the window, her eyes not seeing anything, her brain barely functioning. Demetrius could be in trouble, she thought. La Croix was tough on firearm laws. And Demetrius hadn't just carried a firearm, he'd used it.

She could only pray the police would be lenient.

Arriving at the police station, it didn't take her long to realize the police weren't going to be lenient at all. If anything, they were hostile toward her and refused to let her see Demetrius. "Mr. Mantheakis must be questioned first," the sergeant at the front desk told her.

"His lawyer is coming," she said, trying to stand tall. "You can't question him without his lawyer present."

The sergeant's eyebrows lifted. "Princess Thibaudet, we don't tell you how to run your castle. Please don't try to tell us how to run ours."

There was a derisive note in his voice and she had the peculiar sense that the sergeant was angry with *her*. What had happened? What had she done? "Demetrius Mantheakis works for me. He's my bodyguard—"

"But not just your bodyguard," the sergeant interrupted

rudely. Leaning forward on the desk, he pushed an open newspaper toward her with an elbow.

Her gaze fell, dropping to the open paper. Scandalous Affair! The headlines screamed. Princess Chantal Pregnant With Bodyguard's Baby!

Heat burned through her. Her hand trembled as she gazed at the photo beneath the headlines. It was her in the toilet stall at the cathedral, throwing up.

Anger shot through her, anger and shame that her private life meant so much to tabloid photographers and reporters.

It was disgusting. She was disgusted that people could stoop so low.

"It was my grandmother's funeral," she said quietly, looking up into the sergeant's eyes. "Grief's a difficult thing, isn't it?"

The sergeant had the grace to look chagrined. And Chantal used the silence to make her request again. "I'd like to see my bodyguard now. Please."

The sergeant shifted, less confident than he'd been a few moments earlier. "You can't, Your Highness. Your bodyguard resisted arrest. He's being questioned."

"He didn't resist arrest." Chantal's heart tightened, but she wouldn't let herself feel afraid, wouldn't let herself feel anything but fury. "I was at the scene. I was there. Mr. Mantheakis didn't resist arrest. He did exactly as the officer asked. He cooperated completely."

"I'm sorry. You'll have to wait."

She took a seat in the station, ignoring the glances cast her way, ignoring Alexi standing next to her, ignoring everything but the heaviness in her heart. Demetrius was in serious trouble. She felt it in every pore of her body. There was more to this than a simple arrest. This was payback for a commoner forgetting his place and getting close to a member of the royal family.

She waited an hour. Then two. Her stomach began to get that queasy sick feeling but she wasn't going to leave the station without seeing Demetrius.

"You need to eat," Alexi said quietly.

She shook her head. "Not until I see him." But after waiting three hours, and then four, she knew she had to do something.

She didn't want to involve her family. There was no way she'd have Grandfather or her sisters parading into the police station on her behalf, especially not the day after Grandmama's funeral, but Chantal finally used Alexi's phone to call Nicollette, knowing her sister would still be at the palace in Melio.

"I'm at the police station," she said to Nic. "Demetrius—"

"We've heard. It's all over the news. *Everything* is all over the news."

Chantal closed her eyes. She knew what Nic was saying but didn't have the energy to go into that now. What mattered was Demetrius, and getting Demetrius out of jail. "He did nothing wrong, Nic. He took action to protect me. It was purely self-defense, but I'm worried." Chantal was careful to keep her voice down. "Something's not right. I can feel it in my bones."

"Let me put Malik on the phone. He's right here. He wants to talk to you."

"Chantal?" It was Malik's deep voice and he sounded reassuringly calm. "How is it there?"

"Demetrius is in trouble." She couldn't waste time on preliminary greetings. She was too tired, too heartsick.

"Sounds like it. Tell me what's happened so far."

Chantal gave Nicolette's husband a brief rundown of events, exactly as they unfolded, concluding with Demetrius's arrest and her visit to the station. "They say this is about firearms and resisting arrest, but that's not it, Malik. This is about La Croix national pride. They're punishing Demetrius for consorting with a member of the royal family."

"I think you're right."

Shaking, she rubbed her temple. She knew La Croix's culture and politics better than anyone. "He needs a good lawyer."

"I've already sent one. He should be there soon."

"Thank you." She felt a rush of gratitude. "I appreciate it, Malik."

"It's nothing, Chantal. Take care of yourself, and call us as soon as you've more information."

She'd just hung up the phone when a detective appeared at the front. "You have fifteen minutes, Your Royal Highness," he said to Chantal. "Follow me."

Alexi wanted to come but they wouldn't let him. "I'll be fine," she assured the young bodyguard, before following the detective down a gray hallway into an even more gray conference room with a wood table and folding metal chairs. The detective motioned for her to sit. Chantal glanced at the straggle of folding chairs. Paint was peeling off one. The chairs looked so hard and cold.

"Are you going to question me?" she asked, throat dry, sitting down in the chair nearest her.

"No." The detective turned to leave. "There's no need. We have all the information we need."

The door opened again five minutes later and Chantal sat frozen in her chair as Demetrius was escorted into the room, his hands still cuffed behind him.

She stared at him as if she'd never seen him before. Indeed, she'd never seen him like this before.

What had they done to him?

His face was so puffy she could barely distinguish his features, his right eye nearly swollen closed. Blood oozed from an ugly gash on his cheek.

Her heart rose up to her throat. This couldn't be him. He didn't look like anyone she knew at all. "Demetrius." She whispered his name like a prayer, and her eyes, so dry all day, burned hotter, grittier. There were no tears left to cry.

He stared at her as if she were a stranger, no emotion on his face, and the officer leading him into the room gave Demetrius a small push from behind, thrusting him closer to the table and chipped folding chairs.

She saw him stiffen, his jaw thicken as he ground his teeth together in silent protest.

It was Demetrius all right. And yet the knowledge only ate at her, and she sagged in her chair beneath the weight of her shock. Had she done this to him? He'd only been protecting her. He'd put his body between her and Stefano, drawn a gun only after Stefano had drawn his, and yet she couldn't help feeling guilty. If he hadn't tried to save her...

She knew she being illogical, but she also knew the police would have never treated a member of the royal family this way.

They would have never done this to her father. Her cousin. Her late husband. They couldn't have done this to a member of the royal family and gotten away with it.

"Sit down," the officer said roughly. "And Your Highness, you are not allowed to touch him. There is to be no contact between you."

She must have nodded. She felt her head bob but she could think of nothing, look at nothing, but Demetrius. She watched as he slowly sat. His long, powerful legs were braced in front of him and his arms awkwardly cuffed behind him. "What have they done to you?"

He couldn't answer her. He hurt, badly, but it wasn't the physical pain that kept him silent. He'd been hurt worse before, taken a couple beatings before he left the Family, but what he felt now was different. His pain was alive. And it was in his mind...his heart.

He'd succeeded in protecting the princess but at what cost?

"What have they done?" she repeated.

He heard the quaver in her voice and knew she was afraid right now. Afraid for him, afraid for them, and he wanted to smile for her, wanted to show that he was above all this, but his jaw ached and he couldn't move his lips.

"They can't do this," she whispered fiercely.

He smiled on the inside, smiled without any warmth or humor. "They already have," he said through clenched teeth. His jaw throbbed. His face felt huge, prehistoric, like an excavated dinosaur bone.

She scooted forward in her chair, hands on the table. "We'll get you out. We'll make them pay—"

"Chantal." He said her name hard, sharp, to get her attention. "La Croix is very strict about firearms. I'm not going to get out anytime soon."

"I'll help you."

"How?" His dark eyes searched hers. Abruptly he leaned forward, his big chest coming into contact with the table. "Forget about me, Princess. What you need to do now is get on with your life. Enjoy your daughter. Enjoy the time you have with her. You only get one chance at this, *pedhaki mou*. Make it mean something.''

Was he serious? Forget about him? She was carrying his child. She loved him. She'd never forget him and yet time was up, nothing more could be said. The detective escorted her back to the lobby where Alexis waited.

Moments later they were enroute to the Thibaudet châteaux. She'd only been gone a month, Chantal thought as she stepped through the châteaux's doors, but it seemed so much longer. She didn't feel like family anymore, but a stranger as she climbed the staircase to the nursery on the third floor.

Entering the bright yellow room, Lilly flung herself into her mother's arms and Chantal held her daughter tightly. Some of the wretched emotion bottled inside her escaped and tears seeped from beneath her lids.

''*Mama,*'' Lilly said, squeezing Chantal even harder.

It'd been such a horrible day. Such a horrible week. But she had Lilly in her arms now and that's all that mattered. ''Hello, my darling.'' She stroked Lilly's soft light brown curls, felt her small straight back, marveled at how much her daughter had grown in the month she'd been gone. And holding her she was again amazed how fast the last four years had passed. It didn't seem very long since Lilly was a newborn.

She was still sitting with Lilly in the nursery, holding her on her lap and catching up on everything that had happened—all the events big and small, including the hurts that had loomed huge in Lilly's mind—when the door opened and Queen Catherine Thibaudet stood in the nursery doorway still wearing her beige wool traveling coat.

''We'd like a word with you, Chantal.'' Catherine's voice was crisp, no-nonsense. ''Phillipe is already waiting in his study.''

Dread rushed through Chantal, filling every nerve and pore, weighting her limbs so she trembled a little as she held Lilly. Catherine left and Lilly, sensing Chantal's fear wrapped her arms around her mother's neck. ''Don't be afraid, Mama.''

''I'm not,'' Chantal answered, hating that her daughter should already be aware of her fears. It was her responsibility to protect Lilly, not the other way around. Adults were meant to shield children from stress, to ensure they weren't exposed to things they couldn't handle. For God's sake, it was the adult's job to be the adult.

She dropped a kiss on Lilly's head and ruffled her curls, aiming to lighten the mood. "I'll be back soon."

Phillipe and Catherine were waiting for her in Phillipe's study. They were both seated, sharing a late-afternoon tea.

Catherine motioned for Chantal to sit. Chantal gingerly took a seat, knowing that whatever would follow would be miserable.

"Your grandmama's funeral was lovely," Catherine said, breaking the tense silence. "I'm very glad we were able to attend. I knew your grandmother when I was just a little girl. She was already betrothed to your grandfather." The queen struggled to smile, lips pinching. "I admired her very much."

"Thank you." Chantal had heard this a hundred times. This was the way Armand's parents prefaced everything. *Because of the family ties, out of family respect, due to family loyalty...*and of course, whatever followed was bitter and painful. "It's been a very difficult few days."

Phillipe made a hoarse sound as he cleared his throat. "You can imagine our distress on opening the papers this morning. There we were in your family home in Melio, reading a shocking story about—" He broke off, jaw tightening, pale blue eyes narrowing as he focused on a point below Chantal's hips, somewhere between her ankles and knees, "your bodyguard." He swallowed. "Which, I might add, we didn't understand the necessity of you having in the first place."

"I'm certain the Melio palace detectives made you aware of their investigation," Chantal said quietly, refusing to be baited. She knew how Phillipe worked. He'd try to corner her, intimidate her, frustrate her. But it wouldn't work today. "Just as I'm certain you're aware of Tanguy's death earlier this month—"

"Most tragic, yes," Phillipe interrupted, "but these things happen with cars and such."

How could he say that? These things didn't happen. These things were made to happen, and the fact that Phillipe was going to pretend that Tanguy's death was just a random event sickened Chantal.

But she didn't let her outrage show, didn't let any emotion show. She knew too well how Phillipe preyed on weakness. This time, she vowed, she'd show none. "As you've already heard, my bodyguard, Demetrius Mantheakis, saved my life today." She spoke calmly, her voice firm, controlled. "And yet he's in jail facing ludicrous charges." Never mind that he'd been beaten, she thought, trying to suppress the picture of him in her head, his handsome face bruised and swollen. "I want him released immediately."

"That's impossible." Phillipe answered with an equally firm voice. "He committed a crime—"

"Protecting me."

"I'm sorry, my dear. This must be a very trying time for you." Catherine's lightly penciled eyebrows arched. "Now tell us, is there any truth to the story in this morning's paper? You aren't actually pregnant, are you?"

Chantal went cold on the inside. She felt her lips curve but didn't know whether it was a smile or tears.

"Because you know, dear, that's not permitted, not at all permitted." Catherine was trying hard to interject warmth into her voice but her eyes were brittle and her features were rigid and Chantal wondered how it was she'd survived at the chateaux all these years. These weren't warm people, loving people, but ice royals.

"You can't think you'll be able to keep the baby, Chantal, dear. It's just not possible," Catherine added before she and Phillipe exchanged glances. "He's a common man—"

"And a criminal," Phillipe interrupted. "A member of the Greek mafia—"

"No."

"Son of the mob boss himself," the king continued starkly, "It's speculated that he's been part of numerous unsolved crimes."

"I don't believe it."

"Then have a look at this." Anger flared in the king's voice, and drawing a newspaper from the side table he tossed it at her.

Chantal awkwardly caught it, pages slipping half hazardly this way and that. But she didn't need the middle pages. The information Phillipe wanted her to see was right there, on the front page: Greek Mobster Seduces Princess, was the headline and beneath the dark ink was a black and white photo of Demetrius taken years ago. He was dressed in a dark suit, attending a funeral.

"That's your bodyguard." Phillipe's voice came out in ice chips, hard, sharp, frigid. "And that was his wife. Killed by a warring mafia faction. Read all about it and then tell me I'm *wrong*."

CHAPTER FOURTEEN

"I DON'T need to read it. I know the facts."

"Do you?" Phillipe leaned forward, stared at her so long and hard that she felt almost ugly, shameful. She didn't understand how he could do that to her. Was it the contempt in his eyes? The ridicule in his voice?

But she was tired of feeling ashamed, tired of the pain and stillness and silence. "I do," she answered quietly, clinging to her dignity. "Maybe you are the one that needs to get your facts straight."

Chantal rose then, but she took the paper with her, carrying it back to her room.

She believed in Demetrius. She believed in him with her whole heart but that didn't stop her from wanting to know more. From wanting to know everything.

Hands shaking, she spread the paper flat on her bed and forced herself to read each agonizing word.

He'd been married, just as he'd told her, and his wife had been pregnant. A rival mob kidnapped Demetrius's wife—

Chantal had to stop reading for a moment, had to draw a breath. Her heart had begun to pound and she felt sick inside, sick and afraid even though the events had happened years ago. Because this wasn't just anyone. This was Demetrius. His world, his wife.

Fighting her revulsion, Chantal struggled to read on, knowing that it was only going to get worse, knowing that what she was going to read would break her heart.

Twenty-three-year-old Katina Mantheakis was held for ransom, and even though Demetrius paid the ransom—paid more than was demanded—the rival mob killed Katina Mantheakis anyway.

Despite the fact that she was pregnant. Despite the fact she just weeks from giving birth to a baby girl.

My God.

Chantal squeezed her eyes closed, awash with pain. The story was brief and yet so violent, so horrible that it cut her deeply.

No wonder Demetrius didn't discuss his past. She didn't blame him. Not in the least.

And suddenly, so many things made sense, so much became clear.

The island sanctuary.

The devoted families that lived there.

Demetrius's insistence on protecting her at all costs.

No wonder he didn't trust himself anymore. No wonder he wanted others on the job. She wasn't just a princess, but the mother of his child. His child. And no wonder he needed this child. He wanted to be a father again. Wanted the chance to live again.

And she wanted that for him. She wanted him to have the life, and the family, he'd been denied. But to give him what he needed...what he deserved...meant giving up Lilly.

Could she do it?

Did she have the strength to let one child go to save the other?

Chantal didn't sleep, the hours creeping by, one agonizing minute after another. She left her bed once in the night, went to Lilly's room on the third floor and opened her daughter's door.

A small yellow night-light glowed on the little green painted dresser. In the soft yellow light Lilly's small face glowed. She looked calm. Peaceful.

Chantal's chest squeezed, knotting into a small hard ball. *How do I leave you?* She whispered silently, her eyes burning, too dry now for tears.

And yet her hand moved to her tummy and she placed her palm protectively against her belly. *How do I deny you a chance to live?*

This time her eyes did fill with tears and she pressed her knuckled fist against her face, pressed against her eyes, pressed against the pain.

She had to make a choice. She had to make the right choice. *God, help me do what I must do.*

The long night finally ended and Chantal was in the middle of dressing when she received a message that the Thibaudets wished to see her again.

They were requesting her company at the breakfast table. Lilly, Chantal discovered on arriving in the sunny glass-walled breakfast room, wasn't there.

Taking her place at the formal table, Chantal began to realize how little she saw of her daughter. How much Phillipe and Catherine dictated Lilly's life.

But Phillipe and Catherine were smiling at her now, a unified, almost benevolent smile.

"Good morning, Chantal," Catherine said, starting the conversation as she usually did. "We hope you slept better than we did." She paused, drew a breath. "As you can imagine, we've been talking. We've had a great deal to discuss. This doesn't have to become ugly," she added with her surreal calm and control. "You can put this whole sordid affair behind you right now."

"That's right. Act now, and this—" the king exchanged sly glances with his wife "—can all be dealt with. Quickly. Quietly."

Neatly, Chantal concluded, trying hard to keep her expression blank. They wanted her to get rid of the baby. Turn her back into Armand's devoted widow. Pretend nothing had changed, that nothing would ever change.

"Everyone makes mistakes." The queen was smiling, warmly. Confidently. Her smile seeming to say, we're both girls. We understand these things, we understand how these things can happen, don't we? "We want to help you, Chantal. Dear. More than anything we want to make things right for you and Lilly."

The king leaned across the table to cover Chantal's hand with his. But his hand felt hard, almost punishing and Chantal went cold inside. He was just like Armand. Too much like Armand. He'd ruled with a heavy hand, an iron fist throughout his forty odd years on the throne.

She slid her hand out from beneath her father-in-law's. "And Demetrius?" she asked. "What about him?"

The queen's smile slipped. The king leaned back a fraction in his chair. "He'll serve his time, of course."

His time. The way the king said the words made her blood boil. My God, what did 'his time' mean? And who the hell was Phillipe to impose his law onto others? "He was my bodyguard. He was protecting me."

"You know the law. Unless you have a firearm permit from the government, you can't carry a weapon. Concealed or not."

Chantal almost pounded on the table. "He saved my life."

"Dear, do you really believe that?" The queen's expression had hardened, then softened, and now she gazed at Chantal with something between pity and disbelief. "Do you honestly think you were ever in any danger? Or could it be, my dear, that you are simply too sensitive, stressed by the events around you?"

Chantal shook her head, a slow decisive shake. She wasn't going to sit here and listen to this. She'd spent nearly ten years of her life being lectured, controlled, coerced. She'd had enough. She'd had more than enough. "If you'll excuse me," she said, pushing away from the table. "I have things to do."

Chantal met with the lawyer Malik had sent at the lawyer's hotel downtown. "I'm afraid I don't have good news," the lawyer said regretfully. "La Croix laws are rigid, as well as archaic. There isn't much legal ground for us to stand on."

Chantal had been pacing back and forth in front of the brocade sofa. "If Demetrius were royal, this would have never happened. They'd never prosecute a member of the royal family like this."

"But he's not a member of the family. And you're right, there is a bias. But the bias is aimed at you as much as Mr. Mantheakis. As the mother of the future queen of La Croix, you're being held to a different standard. You're to be above reproach."

"And I have been. For nine years I've done everything they've asked of me and how has it benefited anyone? I rarely see my daughter. I'm not allowed to make decisions for her. I'm barely her mother." Chantal's eyes felt hot, scalding and she knew it was the nights of lost sleep, the weeks of fear, the years of loneliness. "But things have changed. *I've* changed. I'm pregnant."

"You don't have to keep the baby." The lawyer slid his glasses back on, picked up a sheath of papers. "No one would know if you terminated the pregnancy. You could call it a miscarriage—"

"No."

"Demetrius thinks you should."

Her body jerked. *"What?"*

"He wants you to do what is best for you. He wants you to do what is best for Lilly."

The prickling behind her eyes made it difficult to see. "I don't believe that for a moment. He wants this baby." The emotion was too strong, her insides churning, the nausea returning. "And I want this baby, too."

"You might want to think on this some more. I've had a look at the contract you signed. There's no way you can have the baby and remain in La Croix. And if you leave, you won't be able to take Lilly with you."

"Maybe that's what I should do." No matter what she did, the Thibaudets would block her, contain her, control her. Even if she ended the pregnancy, they'd still remember, they'd still be ashamed of her. "I'm tired of living like this. I'm done living like this."

She closed her eyes, tried to imagine her future without her daughter, felt the horrible flood of grief and sorrow and nearly recoiled. She couldn't imagine living without Lilly but she couldn't imagine remaining at the châteaux after terminating the pregnancy, knowing Demetrius was paying an unholy price for doing his job.

"They'd still have to let me see her sometimes," Chantal said quietly. "Holidays. Formal occasions."

"It wouldn't be the same as living under the same roof with her."

"No." She stared across the hotel room, trying to see a future without Lilly there every day.

And suddenly she saw it. She knew what she needed to do. Calm swamped Chantal, calm and focus. She knew what she needed to do. "I have an idea," she said. "But I'm going to need your help. King Nuri's, too."

A day passed, night fell, and after another long sleepless night on his cot, morning came. He'd been in the jail three days, two nights. Yesterday had been quiet, no word from the outside, nothing more from the lawyer Malik Nuri had hired. Now it was a new day but nothing felt new.

Footsteps sounded in the corridor, the footsteps ringing extra loud off all the cement walls. The footsteps stopped outside his cell. Demetrius sat up on his cot as the door to his cell squeaked open.

"What's happening?" he asked, shooting the officer a wary look.

"You're wanted in the interrogation room."

"Again?"

The officer shrugged as he cuffed Demetrius. Trailing the man down the corridor, Demetrius tried to rake a hand through his hair, but the handcuffs made even that difficult. It'd been a long night. It'd be an even longer day. He hated not being near Chantal, not knowing how she was, how she was feeling. He just wanted her safe. Happy. She deserved to be happy.

The officer opened the door to the interrogation room, unlocked Demetrius's handcuffs and pushed him into the room. "You've got ten minutes, Mantheakis."

The door closed behind him with a bang. He winced at the loud sound.

"How's the head?" a quiet voice asked behind him.

Demetrius stiffened, turned, faced Chantal. He'd missed her, but he didn't want her here. It'd only make it harder for her. The press would only print more vicious things. "You shouldn't have come."

She didn't look abashed. If anything she looked cool, controlled. "Really?"

"There's nothing you can do to help me now."

"That's not how I see it," she answered calmly. "I think there's quite a bit I can do." She gestured to the gentleman in dark robes seated at the table. "Demetrius, meet Bishop Kazantzakis."

Bishop Kazantzakis? The bishop from the Greek Orthodox Church in Athens? "What are you doing, Chantal?" Demetrius bit out the words, pulse quickening, anger surging through him. He recognized her expression, saw the light of battle in her eyes, but she shouldn't be fighting for him. She should be fighting for her.

"I'm doing what I should have done before." She glanced at her watch. "We don't have much time. So let's get this going. Bishop?"

"Chantal."

She closed the distance between them, moving so close that he felt heat flare through him, heat, desire, possession. She looked beautiful, regal, dressed in a fine crepe suit the softest cream, immaculate pale hose, pale heels, her dark hair coiled at her nape.

"You're not the only one who knows right and wrong," she said, and her blue eyes flashed, bolts of fire in the sapphire. "I know right and wrong, and I know I can not do what the Thibaudets ask. I know I can not lose this baby, and I can not live without you."

"And I know you. You can't lose Lilly."

Her small firm chin lifted, her full lips pressed giving her classic bone structure the grace and beauty of the ancient Greeks. "I won't lose her. I just won't see her as often. I'm not dying, Demetrius. I'm simply divorcing the Thibaudets."

It felt as if a nail was being driven through his heart. His features tightened, a spasm of pain. He couldn't believe she'd do this for him. He didn't want her to do this for him. Unable to help himself, he reached for her, cupped her pale face, buried his fingers in the coil of hair at her nape. "It'll cost you, *pedhaki mou.*"

Her eyes shone, liquid blue. "And when hasn't it? Being born royal has cost me dearly, every day of my life."

He felt something wild break loose in him, the same thing he'd felt that first night on the beach in Sao Tome. She was breaking his heart. Making him feel an ungodly amount of pain. "I was supposed to protect you," he said hoarsely, his thumb brushing her mouth. "I would have done anything to protect you—"

"You did. You put your life before mine." She struggled to smile but her lips wouldn't work, the tears too close to the surface. "Now it's my turn to put you first. It's what I want to do. It's what I have to do."

"But Lilly—"

"Is loved." She drew a rough breath, the tears clinging to her black lashes. "Her grandparents will always adore her. They'll always be there for her. And so will I. I just won't be there every morning. I just won't be there every night."

"Chantal."

She stood up, pressing close, and covered his mouth with her hand. "Please. This is hard, but it's right. It *is* right. I have a baby inside me, a baby that wants to be born. I have a man I love and he deserves to be a father—" she broke off, bit her lip, fighting for control. "Please, we don't have much time."

Demetrius's eyes burned. His heart burned. He felt as if his body was on fire. "I love you."

She nodded, tears falling. "I know."

He wiped the tears from her face. Her skin was cool, the tears were warm. He couldn't imagine what she'd been going through these past twenty-four hours. He couldn't imagine the soul searching and what it took to come to this decision. "I'd do anything for you," he said, covering her tear-streaked mouth with his own.

Chantal's eyes closed as his tender kiss turned fierce. His desire for her couldn't be contained. It was too strong, too explosive, too much a part of him.

The kiss deepened, and it was like breathing she thought, her arms wrapping around his neck. This was the way it was meant to be. Him, her, them, together. A kiss for a kiss. Air for air. One life for another.

She pressed her hand against his chest, her heart melting, the impossible heat building. "I don't want to be without you," she whispered, turning her lips to brush his beard roughened cheek. "I can't be without you. I can't look at a future without you."

His thumb stroked the side of her face, following the curve of her temple, cheekbone, jawbone. "You're strong. You're stronger than you know."

"I'm stronger than *you* know. I won't let you go. I can survive anything as long as I have you."

He lifted his head, emotion blazing in his eyes. "The Thibaudets will make this miserable for you."

Her lips curved and she felt a welling of intense love. "Maybe. Maybe not. And I'll have the press on my side. They love a good story. We're giving them a story." She saw the flicker in his eyes and her insides were dissolving, love, passion, tenderness. "I'm not afraid of anything anymore. I'm ready to face the world, ready to face the truth. Life is to be lived. I want to live. And I want to live it with you."

"Chantal," he whispered her name deep in his throat and it was strangled, guttural, a sound of pure pain. He was in his own private hell now. "Since Katina died I've wanted nothing for myself. I still want nothing but for you to be happy—"

"Then make me Mrs. Mantheakis," she interrupted. "That would make me happy. I promise."

Bishop Kazantzakis opened his prayer book and in the few minutes they had left, performed the shortest, simplest wedding ceremony ever. There was no time for scripture verses, no time for a homily, there were just the vows, the exchange of rings Chantal had brought with her, and then the blessing. But it was, Chantal thought as the Bishop placed his hand on their joined hands, the most beautiful wedding ever.

"In the power vested to me by God and the Greek Orthodox Church, I now pronounce you man and wife," the Bishop concluded.

Chantal stepped into Demetrius's arms, and kissed him, giving him all her heart, giving him everything she'd ever dreamed, everything she'd ever felt.

The door to the interrogation room opened. The detective had returned. "Time's up."

Chantal stood on tip toe and kissed Demetrius one last time, trying to smile through her tears. "I'll see you soon."

The media were waiting for Chantal outside the La Croix jail. She'd spread the word that something big was going to happen and she used the opportunity as she left the jail to announce that she was no longer Princess Chantal Thibuadet, but Mrs. Demetrius Mantheakis. "As soon as my husband's freed we plan on returning to Greece."

She was done being on the defensive, she thought, sliding into the back of the waiting limousine. From now on she was on the offensive. She was taking control.

But it was one thing to announce her marriage to the eager, story-hungry media; it was another to face the furious Thibaudets.

The chateaux was in an uproar when she arrived, and Chantal was ushered none too gently into a downstairs salon. "What in God's name have you done?" Catherine demanded, voice shaking. "We were going to *help* you. We were going to *fix* this—"

"I didn't want it *fixed*," Chantal interrupted fiercely. She was pregnant. Her beloved grandmother had died. And instead of sympathy, or support, her in-laws were bullying her. Belittling her. Making her life a living hell. "I wanted to do what was right. And I did it."

"Right?" Phillipe repeated, outraged. "Marrying a Greek criminal isn't right. And holding a press conference outside the jail was unthinking...selfish. Have you given a thought in all this to Lilly? Have you even considered *our* feelings?"

"Yes." Chantal straightened, and she realized she was done cowering, done biting her tongue, forever done with running away. "Your feelings are all I ever seem to think about. And I've thought this through, and I know this will impact Lilly, but Lilly can handle this. Lilly's smart, and loving, and she's not going to lose me."

"Wrong." Catherine marched toward her, her slim body shaking. "She did just lose you. Because you're gone. You're out of here now. You'll never see her again."

"You can't keep me from her." Chantal held her ground. "I'm her mother, and I do have rights. No government anywhere would deny me time with her. So maybe she will live here, go to school here, but she'll have weekends and holidays with me."

The salon doors burst open. Demetrius entered the room. He'd showered, shaved, and dressed in a dark suit, and he was accompanied by Nicolette and King Nuri. Nicolette was carrying Lilly, and Lilly looked delighted to be in the arms of her favorite aunt.

"What's this?" Phillipe demanded. "What are you all doing here?"

"Taking Chantal and Lilly home," Demetrius answered, joining Chantal. He shot her a quizzical glance. His way of checking on her.

Chantal would have smiled if she weren't so stunned. "What are you doing here?"

"I think, for once, you have to be thankful to the media. Charges were dropped," he said. "The police chief took pity on me."

"But that doesn't explain what you're doing here," Phillip said, red-faced, agitated. "And it doesn't change Lilly's status. As heir—"

"But she's not heir," King Nuri interrupted evenly. "She's not even your legitimate grandchild."

Chantal couldn't have been more shocked. She rocked back on her heels, absolutely stunned. *"What?"*

Demetrius indicated Phillipe. "He knows," Demetrius said. "He knows your marriage was never legal because Armand's first marriage was never properly annulled."

Armand had a first marriage? There was a first wife somewhere?

"Armand has a son from the first marriage, too. A boy who is almost nine. The boy should be La Croix's heir, not Lilly." Demetrius looked at Chantal, expression strained. "I'm sorry, Chantal."

Philippe's mouth opened, closed. "The first marriage was dissolved. The annulment is nothing but a technicality."

"Just like the prenuptial contract is just a technicality, too?" King Nuri's asked slyly.

There was a moment of strained silence and then Phillipe spoke. "We don't even recognize this other marriage. We never approved of the woman, and have never accepted the son—"

"Too bad. Because he's a really nice kid. A smart, polite kid who could have benefited from loving grandparents."

Catherine pressed her hand to her mouth. Phillipe just looked enraged. "I have a granddaughter and heir. She's right here, right now."

"We love Lilly," Catherine chimed faintly. "We love our baby."

Chantal moved toward Nicollete, whispered in her sister's ear, asking Nic to take Lilly from the room before the scene became even more upsetting for her daughter.

Chantal waited until Nic was gone and the salon doors were closed to answer Catherine. "But she's not your baby," Chantal said. "She's my baby. And you've done everything in your power to take her from me."

Catherine reached out to Chantal. "But we need her—"

"No," Chantal interrupted. "You don't need her. At least not the way you think. She's just a little girl. Why can't she be a little girl?"

"Wait. Stop." Phillipe cleared his throat, obviously struggling to regain control over his emotions. "Can't we discuss this rationally? Let's sit down like reasonable people and talk this out properly."

But there was nothing reasonable or rational left in Chantal. She'd been through hell and back for what? She'd been trapped here for years for what?

"Talk?" Chantal repeated tiredly. "Don't you think, Phillipe, it's a little late to *talk?*"

"Chantal!" Catherine's voice broke. "Please, dear, please."

Chantal held her breath, concentrated on slowing her racing heart. She didn't want to hurt them, and she didn't want to hurt Lilly. "I won't keep her from seeing you. You'll always be her grandparents, but she belongs with me." Chantal shot Demetrius a grateful glance. "She belongs home with us."

They returned that same evening to Demetrius's island in Greece, and back at the large villa with the breathtaking view of the sea, Chantal felt some of the horrendous tension in her shoulders begin to ease.

With Lilly tucked into bed, she and Demetrius faced each other outside on the moon lit terrace. "So much has happened today," she said. "I can't believe we're here. Can't believe we're together—"

"Can't believe we're married?"

She heard the hard note in his voice and grinned a little mischievously. "You imagine I have regrets?"

"You might. It was a rather hasty decision."

Chantal laughed. She couldn't help it. She was feeling so much lighter, the pressure on her chest gone, her breathing easy. "And if I did have regrets, would you let me go?"

"No."

He answered so sharply, so crossly that she laughed again, the sound tinkling like wind chimes. "You're in a bad mood, Mr. Mantheakis."

He glared at her, his jaw still bruised but not quite as swollen. "If you weren't pregnant," he growled, shaking his head.

Her eyes danced. She felt happy, naughty, wicked. "And what would you do?"

"I'd pull you onto my lap and take you here." His dark eyes burned, desire evident in the tightness of his features, in the deepening of his voice. "I'd have you, and make love to you, until you could think of nothing but me."

She leaned toward him, brushed her lips across his cheekbone, near his ear. "So what's stopping you?"

He reached up, captured her face between his hands, fingers twining tight in her long loose hair. "I'm not in a sensitive mood, *pedhaki mou*."

She nipped his earlobe with her teeth. "Good. Neither am I."

"*Chantal.*" His voice deepened yet again, the inflection painfully husky.

Arching against him, she let him feel her breasts, the length of her abdomen, the curve of hips. "Take me. Right here. Right now."

She felt rather than heard the hiss of air as he exhaled, his fingers sliding from her hair, his hands slipping down her shoulders, pressing firmly against her flesh until he'd encircled her waist. "I don't want to hurt you."

"Hurt me?" She lifted her arms, slid them around his neck and kissed him, lightly, playfully, letting her tongue flick his upper lip, feeling the firmness, tasting the wine he'd had at dinner. "You'd never hurt me. Not in a thousand years. I trust you with my life."

His fingers kneaded her hip. "Careful, *pedhaki mou*, you don't want to see a grown man cry."

She pressed even closer to him, and she kissed him more

deeply, offering all of herself to him, offering all of the love in her heart, love that had never been wanted before, love that had never been needed. "Why not?" she whispered, her heart like that of the mythical phoenix, the beautiful bird rising from the ashes. "A few tears never hurt anyone."

"It's not manly," he protested, blinking fiercely.

Her lips curved and gently she reached up, wiped his lashes dry. "There. Strong and manly as ever." And then her own eyes filled with tears. She stared up at him, speechless, heart brimming over, her world so changed she couldn't even take it all in. "You saved me."

"No."

"Yes, Demetrius. You set me free." And she struggled to smile. "I'm free."

He made a rough sound, a little indignant, rather impatient. "I wouldn't call it free. You are married to me."

And Chantal kissed him, the happiness so strong, her lightness so intense, she felt dangerous, wicked all over again. "So prove it to me." She looked into his eyes, daring him, challenging him, wanting to provoke him as much as she could. "Now."

Groaning, swallowing curses, he swept her into his arms, carried her through the house, up the stairs to his bedroom, a room she'd never been in before. It was at the very top of the house, a massive suite with windows on all four walls, windows that captured every view of the island imaginable. Earth, sky, mountain, sea. The moon light bathed the rugged landscape, painting the ground and sea shades of silver and white.

"You're in trouble now," he said, dropping her none too gently on the bed.

"Good."

"Good?" he mocked, his hooded gaze growing hard and hot as he watched her sprawl backward, long brown hair tumbling over her shoulders, skirt hiking high on her thigh. "You might want to rethink that answer."

"Never."

He leaned forward, pushed her skirt up higher until her cream lace panty was revealed, and then slowly, deliberately parted her knees.

She blushed, growing so warm she felt feverish.

He was watching her face, saw her bite her lip. ''I think you like living dangerously,'' he said, hand on her knee, feeling her body tremble with excitement.

''Of course. I've got you around to protect me.''

He moved forward, stretching out above her, weight propped on his elbows. ''And who, *pedhaki mou,* will protect you from me?''

Her eyes felt so heavy. Her body tingled. Her blood felt sweet and hot. It was like she'd been sipping champagne but she'd had nothing to drink.

It was love.

It was joy.

It was life itself.

She smiled, lips curving with delicious intent, and reaching up, she tugged on his shirt, pulling the tails from his trousers. ''So are you just going to talk, Demetrius Mantheakis, or are you actually going to make love to me?''

She helped strip him and then he lowered his weight until the hard planes of his body touched hers. She sighed at the feel of his bare chest, the strength of his corded thighs, the hard press of his erection to her inner thigh. ''I had no idea you enjoyed sex this much,'' he mocked her, dipping his head to kiss her neck, then her collarbone before his lips caressed the swell of her breast and closed over one aching nipple.

She gasped as he kissed her through the thin silk of her blouse. His mouth seared her, his mouth so warm, making her skin burn, her body melt, the core of her damp.

''Now,'' she choked, dragging her hands through his thick, crisp hair, finger nails raking his scalp. ''I want you *now.*''

He made a rough *tsk-tsking.* ''You think I'm going to rush this? Sorry, *agaope mou,* I'm not about to hurry anything. You're mine, remember? And what is mine, I cherish and protect.''

And that, she thought breathing hard and fast as his hand slid beneath her skirt, beneath her lace panty, was all she could ask for.

By the time he'd peeled the last of her clothes from her warm, flushed body she was trembling all over, her breath trapped in her chest, her imagination stirred. He entered her slowly, so slowly that she needed his kiss to help her remember to breathe. He'd been an incredible lover their first night together, but tonight, their first night as husband and wife he was beyond great, beyond brilliant, he was perfectly wonderfully hers.

Her lover. Her heart. Her future.

Chantal couldn't hold back the tears as he took her to a place she'd never dreamed existed. She didn't understand how it'd happened. One moment she'd been on a silver plane falling from the heavens, and the next moment she was on a shooting star, soaring back across the sky. It was the trip of a lifetime, the most incredible experience.

"Thank you." She pressed her tear-streaked face against his smoothly muscled shoulder, her body still rippling from the aftershocks of their lovemaking. "Thank you from the bottom of my heart."

Demetrius lifted his head, stared down into her wet eyes. "Don't thank me."

"I have to." She tried to hold back the emotion and yet she'd never known such overwhelming happiness. It was like she'd swallowed the sun, and it was glowing full and golden inside of her. "We're here because of you. We have what we have because you treated me like a real person...like an ordinary woman."

"You'll never be ordinary."

"But Demetrius, that's all I want, that's all I've ever wanted to be." She pressed her face to his chest, loving the feel of his damp skin against hers, the steady beating of his heart, the strong powerful arms wrapped around her. "I just never thought I'd have this...never thought I'd feel this way."

It always amazed Chantal how Demetrius made love to her. He could be so hard, so fierce during the day but at night, he was completely hers. With his arms around her she knew she'd found everything she'd ever wanted. She'd always loved being a mother, but she'd never known the pleasure of being a wife...a lover.

But he wasn't just good in bed, he was so good in his heart, and she didn't care where he came from, or what his family had been. She knew him, and she believed in him, and being loved like this, and held like this, was all she needed.

Later, as the moon slipped from one end of the sky to the other, Chantal nestled deeper into Demetrius's arms and let out a contented sigh. "It was a lucky break," she murmured, caressing the sinewy muscles of his upper arm, feeling the hard curve of his bicep, the thick cut of his tricep, "learning about Armand's first marriage. How did Malik find out? Did he just discover the truth today?"

Demetrius dropped a kiss on top of her head. "It wasn't Malik. I found out."

"When?"

"Earlier this week, before we left for La Croix."

She lay very still, her brow furrowing, trying to make sense of what he was telling her. He'd known about Armand's first marriage for days.

He'd known but he'd kept it secret.

"Why didn't you tell me?" she whispered.

"You had enough to think about, enough decisions to make without me forcing your hand."

She shook her head, turned in his arms to face him. The moonlight shadowed his profile, creating stark patterns of light and dark on his proud brow and strong nose. "You could have ended up in jail. You could have ended up..." She swallowed. "But why? I don't understand."

He reached up, tucked a tendril of hair behind one ear. "It's easy. I wanted what you wanted."

Emotion grew hot and thick inside her chest, her heart aching at the idea of Demetrius remaining in jail if she hadn't made the decision she did. "But how could you sacrifice yourself like that? You're so important, Demetrius, you matter so much."

"To you."

"Yes." She hated the prickly sting of the tears burning the back of her eyes. "To me. That's right. You matter so much to me."

"Exactly. Which is why we're here, together—"

"But it could have ended so differently!"

He clasped her face, stared at her long and hard with those

dark impenetrable eyes of his. "No. Not for us. There wasn't a chance in hell we wouldn't be together."

He was impossible. Incredible. So unbelievably arrogant. "How can you say that?"

Pulling her down to him, he let their warm bodies come together and his lips cover hers. "Because I'm Greek. And we're an old civilization full of patience and wisdom."

She laughed against his mouth. "Do be serious!"

"Okay. Because I'm Greek and I love you more than life itself. How is that?"

How could he turn her inside out like that? A shiver raced across her skin. Her heart beat double-hard. "Perfect."

EPILOGUE

Four months later...

THEY'D been out by the pool, enjoying the later summer sunshine when Chantal felt the strangest sensation.

It was like a whisper of sensation, a fluttery feeling in her middle and the hair rose on Chantal's arms. Her eyes opened wide. She lay still, and concentrated. After a moment the delicate ripple returned, a caress inside her, and abruptly Chantal sat up in her lounge chair, hands protectively cupping her tummy.

There. Again. Another little flutter...like a paper boat drifting across the water.

"Demetrius." She said his name before she could stop herself.

He looked up from the edge of the pool where he'd been teaching Lilly to swim, and his black brows pulled, immediate worry in his dark eyes. "What's wrong?"

The baby had moved. She'd felt the baby move. Her eyes watered. "Nothing." And she covered her gently swollen stomach with the palm of her hand.

It was real. The baby was real. Her family here on the Rock was real.

Demetrius set Lilly on the edge of the pool, and stared at Chantal, his dark gaze searching her flushed face. "What's happening?"

She didn't think she could explain. Everything was happening. Everything was turning out just as she'd dreamed. Home. Family. Happiness.

The white plaster house with the blue shutters. The laundry singing on a clothesline. The scent of basil and rosemary in the air.

Tomatoes and cucumbers in the garden.

A husband who meant more to Chantal than anything.

A gorgeous healthy, happy five-year-old and a new baby on the way.

How could it be? How could anything be so wonderful, so incredible? How could she finally feel so much warmth and love?

How could it have really come true for her after all the disappointments, all the pain?

How could the world be so good? Because Lilly was happy here, Lilly had taken to Demetrius and the island and the people and Demetrius smiled frequently—even though fools didn't smile—and they'd settled in together as if they'd always meant to be together.

And maybe they had meant to be together.

"Are you all right?" Demetrius climbed from the pool, and was toweling Lilly off, yet his dark gaze never wavered from her face.

"Yes. I'm fantastic." And it was true. She'd never felt so good. She'd never felt anything this lovely in all her life.

It was like a bubble of laughter caught in the middle of her. The laughter rising a little, sinking a little, a hugely buoyant smile that shimmered on the inside.

Chantal wrapped her arms around her knees, hugged herself, hugged the happiness and vowed she'd never let it go. Never. Ever. She'd waited her whole life to feel this way. She'd paid her dues and she'd sacrificed like crazy.

Now she could be happy. Really happy. Even if the rest of the world went mad, she deserved to keep this little bit of joy inside.

It belonged to her. It felt right inside of her. Her whole body was smiling, her heart grinning, little tears in her eyes.

"Come here," she said to Demetrius, and Lilly, extending an arm. "Please."

Demetrius was at her side, a towel wrapped Lilly in his arms. "What is it?"

She laughed, leaned forward, kissed him on the lips. "Your baby." Her eyes burned with a happiness she never thought she'd know, the kind of happiness she thought was reserved for other people. "Your baby just moved. I thought you'd want to know."

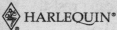

If you enjoyed what you just read,
then we've got an offer you can't resist!

Take 2 bestselling love stories FREE!
Plus get a FREE surprise gift!

"Twisted villains, dangerous secrets...irresistible."
—*Booklist*

New York Times Bestselling Author

STELLA CAMERON

Just weeks after inheriting Rosebank, a once-magnificent Louisiana plantation, David Patin was killed in a mysterious fire, leaving his daughter, Vivian, almost bankrupt. With few options remaining, Vivian decides to restore the family fortunes by turning Rosebank into a resort hotel.

Vivan's dream becomes a nightmare when she finds the family's lawyer dead on the sprawling grounds of the estate. Suddenly Vivian begins to wonder if her father's death was really an accident...and if the entire Patin family is marked for murder.

Rosebank is not in Sheriff Spike Devol's jurisdiction, but Vivian, fed up with the corrupt local police, asks him for unofficial help. The instant attraction between them leaves Spike reluctant to get involved—until another shocking murder occurs and it seems that Vivian will be the next victim.

kiss them goodbye

"Cameron returns to the wonderfully atmospheric Louisiana setting...for her latest sexy-gritty, compellingly readable tale of romantic suspense."—*Booklist*

Available the first week of October 2004, wherever paperbacks are sold!

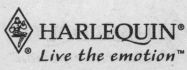

The world's bestselling romance series.

HARLEQUIN®
Presents·

Seduction and Passion Guaranteed!

THE PRINCESS BRIDES

For duty, for money…for passion!

Discover a thrilling new trilogy from a rising star of Harlequin
Presents®, Jane Porter!

Meet the Royals…

Chantal, Nicolette and Joelle are members of the blue-blooded
Ducasse family. Step inside their sophisticated and glamorous
world and watch as these beautiful princesses find they have
to marry three international playboys—for duty, for money…
and definitely for passion!

Don't miss

THE SULTAN'S BOUGHT BRIDE (#2418)
September 2004

THE GREEK'S ROYAL MISTRESS (#2424)
October 2004

THE ITALIAN'S VIRGIN PRINCESS (#2430)
November 2004

**Pick up a Harlequin Presents® novel and you will enter a world
of spine-tingling passion and provocative, tantalizing romance!**

Available wherever Harlequin books are sold.

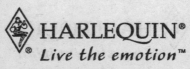

HARLEQUIN®
Live the emotion™

www.eHarlequin.com

HPPBJPOR